Stone Cold

Hannah took another sip of coffee, then said, "I still can't believe your shop club calls themselves the Firing Squad. It's a bit grisly, isn't it?"

I shrugged. "Don't blame me. I didn't pick it."

Hannah's gaze never left mine, so I finally admitted, "Okay, maybe I did suggest it, but I thought it would work well with the name of the shop. Besides, it's not like Betty was shot. Someone used one of my awls on her."

If I closed my eyes, I could still see the wooden handle and just a hint of the sharp steel skewer sticking out of her chest. I decided not to close my eyes, at least until the image had a chance to fade a little bit. If it ever did . . .

A Murderous Glaze

Melissa Glazer

BERKLEY PRIME CRIME, NEW YORK

THE BERKLEY PUBLISHING GROUP
Published by the Penguin Group
Penguin Group (USA) Inc.
375 Hudson Street, New York, New York 10014, USA
Penguin Group (Canada), 90 Eglinton Avenue East, Suite 700, Toronto, Ontario M4P 2Y3, Canada
(a division of Pearson Penguin Canada Inc.)
Penguin Books Ltd., 80 Strand, London WC2R 0RL, England
Penguin Group Ireland, 25 St. Stephen's Green, Dublin 2, Ireland (a division of Penguin Books Ltd.)
Penguin Group (Australia), 250 Camberwell Road, Camberwell, Victoria 3124, Australia
(a division of Pearson Australia Group Pty. Ltd.)
Penguin Books India Pvt. Ltd., 11 Community Centre, Panchsheel Park, New Delhi—110 017, India
Penguin Group (NZ), 67 Apollo Drive, Rosedale, North Shore 0632, New Zealand
(a division of Pearson New Zealand Ltd.)
Penguin Books (South Africa) (Pty.) Ltd., 24 Sturdee Avenue, Rosebank, Johannesburg 2196, South Africa

Penguin Books Ltd., Registered Offices: 80 Strand, London WC2R 0RL, England

This is a work of fiction. Names, characters, places, and incidents either are the product of the author's imagination or are used fictitiously, and any resemblance to actual persons, living or dead, business establishments, events, or locales is entirely coincidental. The publisher does not have any control over and does not assume any responsibility for author or third-party websites or their content.

Kilns, cutting knives, and other craft tools can be hazardous, if used carelessly. All participants in such craft activities must assume responsibility for their own actions and safety. The information contained in this book cannot replace sound judgment and good decision making, which can help reduce risk exposure, nor does the scope of this book allow for disclosure of all the potential hazards and risks involved in such activities.

A MURDEROUS GLAZE

A Berkley Prime Crime Book / published by arrangement with the author

PRINTING HISTORY
Berkley Prime Crime mass-market edition / November 2007

Copyright © 2007 by The Berkley Publishing Group.
Cover art and logo by Robert Crawford.
Cover design by Annette Fiore.
Interior text design by Laura K. Corless.

ISBN: 978-0-425-21836-5

BERKLEY® PRIME CRIME
Berkley Prime Crime Books are published by The Berkley Publishing Group,
a division of Penguin Group (USA) Inc.,
375 Hudson Street, New York, New York 10014.
The name BERKLEY PRIME CRIME and the BERKLEY PRIME CRIME design are trademarks of Penguin Group (USA) Inc.

PRINTED IN THE UNITED STATES OF AMERICA

10 9 8 7 6 5 4 3 2 1

To my editor, Sandy Harding.
With much thanks!

Chapter 1

My name is Carolyn Emerson, and I should probably admit up front that I didn't care for Betty Wickline, not from the first second she stepped into Fire at Will, my paint-your-own-pottery shop. Some customers are like that, generating an instant animosity in me from the moment they walk across my threshold. Now you're probably thinking that I'm a dreadful woman, but you must believe me when I say that I get along perfectly fine with nearly all of my other customers.

Just not Betty.

I told you she was dead, didn't I?

My husband, Bill, swears that I leave out important details sometimes, but it's not true. Not usually, anyway. We've been married twenty-nine years (I was a child bride. Well, I was. All right, I was twenty-three when I had my first, if you must know), we've raised two fine sons, and I've run Fire at Will for the last five years, but my husband still accuses me of being scattered when it comes to relaying all of the pertinent details.

Oh, did I mention Betty was murdered?

Goodness, maybe Bill's right, not that I'd ever admit it to him.

So that's it, all you need to know. Betty Wickline was dead; murdered, in fact.

Oh, there's one more thing. Somehow, the dreadful woman managed to expire in my pottery shop after hours when the place had been shut down for the night.

That's everything. I'm sure of it.

Unless I neglected to mention that John Hodges, the ancient sheriff for Maple Ridge, Vermont—the town where I live—is under the distinct impression that I had something to do with it.

"I can't believe you're taking this so calmly," Hannah Atkins said as we sipped coffee at In the Grounds, a shop that had the most wonderful blends of exotic dry roasts, but the most dreadful name I'd ever heard.

"There's hardly anything I can do about it, is there?" I asked. I'd stumbled across the body the night before, and had enjoyed precious little sleep since. This morning I'd ordered a double jolt of espresso instead of my usual plain black coffee, but it may as well have been water for all the impact it was having on me.

"No, I suppose not," she conceded. "But somehow I didn't imagine we'd be sitting here at our regular table this morning as though nothing happened last night."

"Surely you don't suspect me as well?" I asked. Hannah has been my dear friend for many years. On the surface, we have hardly anything in common. I'm in my early fifties, more than a touch overweight, and have gray hair relentlessly advancing into my natural mousy brown, whereas Hannah is a slim, striking brunette barely over forty. She's an English professor at Travers College—a fine arts institution on the edge of town—and is my assistant David's mother. Despite our differences, she's the best friend I've ever had. Hannah and I meet for coffee whenever we can, except on Sundays, when the place is too crowded to find a spot in line, let alone a table to ourselves. It's our way of staying in touch, a retreat from the insanity of the world around us.

"Of course I know you didn't do it," she replied curtly. I wondered when David's name would come up in our conversation, and it didn't take long. A sudden look of panic flitted across her eyes. "They don't suspect my son, do they?" Her motherly instinct of protecting her only child suddenly kicked into overdrive. "I'm going to get him the best lawyer in Maple Ridge. That's not quite good enough, is it? I'll go to Burlington." She shook her head, paused a moment, then nodded resolutely. "Boston. I'm going to get someone from Boston."

I touched her hand lightly. "Take it easy, Hannah. Nobody has accused David of anything."

She refused to be reassured that easily. "But surely the sheriff talked to him, too, didn't he? After all, David has a key to your place. That means he had access to the murder scene." Hannah shivered as she said the word "murder," and I didn't blame her one bit. It gave me the creeps, too.

"If that's all it takes to be a suspect, there are quite a few other people besides David and me who must be under suspicion."

Hannah took a sip of coffee, then asked, "Carolyn, who else has a key to your shop?"

I pulled a small notebook out of my purse and studied my notes. Sheriff Hodges had asked me the same thing the night before, and I'd been working on my list since then. "First off, there's Robert Owens. He just started teaching at Travers. Have you two met yet?"

"No, but he's already getting a reputation," Hannah said.

That certainly got my attention. "What kind of reputation does he have, and why didn't you say anything before I hired him last week to teach some of my pottery classes?"

"Carolyn, I only heard something the other day about him fraternizing with his students. Actually, it was just the coeds."

"Great, that's just wonderful. That's all I need. Too bad he's still out of town, or I could point the sheriff in his direction."

Hannah tapped the table impatiently with her fingers. "No tangents, Carolyn. Who else is on your list?"

I looked at my notebook and studied the other names I'd written on the pad. Then I promised myself I wouldn't editorialize as I read them. Tangents, indeed.

"So far, I've got Jenna Blake, Martha Knotts, Herman Meadows, and my husband."

She arched one eyebrow. "Why on earth do all of those people need keys to your shop?"

"Jenna and Martha are members of the Firing Squad, and Herman's my landlord. It just makes sense that he'd have his own key. I know I gave Bill one, too, but heaven only knows where that one's hiding."

Hannah took another sip of coffee, then said, "I still can't believe your shop club calls themselves the Firing Squad. It's a bit grisly, isn't it?"

I shrugged. "Don't blame me. I didn't pick it."

Hannah's gaze never left mine, so I finally admitted, "Okay, maybe I did suggest it, but I thought it would work well with the name of the shop. Besides, it's not like Betty was shot. Someone used one of my awls on her." If I closed my eyes, I could still see the wooden handle and just a hint of the sharp steel skewer sticking out of her chest. I decided not to close my eyes, at least until the image had a chance to fade a little bit. If it ever did. I was so thankful that Bill had been with me when I'd discovered the body. After we'd eaten our dinner, I hadn't been able to remember if I'd turned on the pottery kilns before I'd left the shop, and David had an evening class at Travers, so he wouldn't be able to double-check for me. I didn't want to lose a night's firing, so I'd dragged Bill downtown to the shop with me, though he'd grumbled all along the way. The irony was that I must have turned the kilns on after all, though I didn't realize that until after I'd found Betty's body. I'd have to check the pieces when I got to the shop, but I couldn't bring myself to go back there, at least not yet.

"More coffee?" I asked Hannah as I tried to get the attention of our waitress, Cindy Maitland. If David had been with us, we wouldn't have been able to take a sip without her noticing, since Cindy had a major crush on Hannah's son. But we were alone, and apparently invisible as well.

Hannah shook her head. "Sorry, I'd really love to, but I've got to run," she said as she glanced at her watch. "There are young minds waiting to be twisted."

"And no one is better qualified to do that than you," I said with a smile as I reached for the check.

She was quicker, though. "It's my turn, remember? After all, with the night you had, it's the least I can do."

"Thanks," I said as I followed her out of the coffee shop. She headed for the parking lot and I turned toward Fire at Will. It was a beautiful, brisk Vermont morning—the kind I'd always adored—so I decided I'd come back for my car later. Though the temperature in our part of the

state had gotten down into the high twenties the night before, it was nearly forty now, with the weatherman's promise of fifty by afternoon. In fact, if it hadn't been for the
murder the night before, it would have been my perfect
kind of day, even if it was April 15, a date the federal gov-
ernment had ruined for me without actually resorting to
homicide. Despite that single cloud, it was a good day to
walk. I often left my Intrigue in the community lot to save
more parking spaces near the shop for my customers.

Whoever had designed the town of Maple Ridge had
been a visionary. Long before San Antonio's much more
spectacular River Walk, we sported a handful of shops bor-
dering Whispering Brook, a nice creek that flowed through
the center of what passed as our business district, at least
when the water wasn't frozen. Some of the town fathers
had considered adding heating coils to the streambed to
keep the water flowing twelve months a year, but they'd
been voted down at the town meeting and nearly thrown
out of Vermont to boot. For the most part, we liked things
just the way they were, and it was a brave resident who
proposed change during one of our community's monthly
town meetings. There was a narrow strip of lane between
the shops and the water, with just enough parking to make
the shopping agreeable. I liked the way the sidewalk was
wider than the street it serviced.

As I walked beside the water, I glanced at the shops dis-
playing their wares. One of my husband's chairs was in the
window of Shaker Styles. Bill was supposedly retired, but
he built furniture now for Olive Haslett, a hobby that had
quickly become a demanding job. An engineer by trade,
my husband had always been drawn to the elegant lines
and precise joinery of Shaker-style furniture, but it wasn't
until our sons left home that he started building pieces
himself in the workshop in back of our house. Olive had

been delighted when Bill had stepped in after her husband, Jack, the original furniture builder, had passed away, a chisel still resting gently in his hand.

Next up was Rose Colored Glasses, a shop that featured decorative stained glass windows, sun catchers, and such. Rose Nygren peeked out from behind a drawn curtain as I walked by. Was she hiding from me? I was tempted to walk up and pound on her door, but that would probably just fuel speculation around town that I was on some kind of rampage. I hurried my pace as I approached Hattie's Attic, an antique shop that sported high-dollar price tags that would make a robber baron blush. I was hoping I'd miss the owner, Kendra Williams, but no such luck. Her door flew open before I could scurry past.

"Dear, poor, Carolyn. You look dreadful."

"Thanks, Kendra. You're too kind."

I tried to sidestep her, but the old gal was too slick for me. I doubted that Kendra herself knew the original color of her hair. This week it was a ghastly red hue that wasn't found in nature. Her abundant figure was partially hidden by one of the muumuus she habitually wore. This one was a faded print that may have once been beautiful, perhaps in the Civil War.

"Now, dear, you must come inside and tell me all about it. I've got a kettle on."

The last thing I wanted to do was have a tête-à-tête with the village gossip. I knew that even if I didn't give her a single detail about what had happened, the rumors would still fly around Maple Ridge, but at least they wouldn't be based on any information I had provided.

"Sorry, but I've got to get ready to open my shop."

She looked taken aback by the news. "You're actually going to work today? How dreadful." Kendra lowered her voice as she asked, "Is that wise? I'm sure the police need access to your business for their investigation."

"As a matter of fact, they've okayed it." They had, too. Not that John Hodges had done it willingly. He had some deluded idea that he could keep Fire at Will locked up until he solved the murder, but I had dissuaded him of that idea in a heartbeat. I couldn't meet my rent payment if I had to shut the place down, and I wasn't about to lose my business over something I hadn't done.

The sheriff and I had been butting heads for twenty years. He'd once accused my youngest son of vandalism with no proof other than his "gut instinct," as Hodges had called it, and our relationship—while never cordial before— had devolved after that into a strong dislike. I knew I was overly sensitive in my reactions and short-tempered every time I talked to the man, but I couldn't disguise the open contempt I had for him, nor could I suppress it. I was surprised I had convinced him to let me keep the shop open.

I finally got away from Kendra and raced past the other stores, keeping my eyes on the flowing water. Whispering Brook was a lovely name, though not the original moniker. It had been Pig Snout Creek on the earliest survey maps because of a bulge in the stream where an odd pair of islets existed that resembled a hog's nostrils, but even our early forefathers knew that name wasn't going to make folks happy about living in Maple Ridge. So they'd changed it with an alacrity that must have stunned even them. It was one improvement I would have heartily embraced myself. Whispering Brook evoked much nicer images than Pig Snout Creek.

In no time at all, I was standing in front of Fire at Will. There were some pottery pieces for sale in the front plate-glass window display: a lovely set of hand-thrown dishes with a deep green glaze that Robert Owens had created, a unique face jug David had made, a vase with rippling sides thrown on one of my pottery wheels by Martha Knotts—a young mother of five and a member of the Firing Squad—and a set of glazed, hand-cut outdoor ornaments that I had made myself. On the exterior, there was a forest green awning over the tumbled red brick building that sported the shop's name, and a black front door painted the color of midnight. I loved the shop, and hated the fact that someone had used it for a murder.

I started to unlock the front door when I realized it was already unlocked. Taking a deep breath, I steeled myself and walked inside. "Hello? Is anyone here?" I searched for a weapon—anything I could use against an intruder—but there was nothing within reach except a forgotten umbrella in the stand by the door. It was better than nothing, I supposed, so I grabbed it.

"Hello?" I called again. What was I doing? Someone had been murdered in my shop last night, and here I was, armed only with an umbrella, preparing to confront a prowler. What an idiot I could be sometimes. I started to back out of the shop so I could call the sheriff when a familiar face popped out of the back room.

"Is it raining, Carolyn?"

My assistant, David, had never looked so handsome to me in his life. Twenty years old, David was slim like his mother, but instead of brunette hair, he was blond—just like his dad—though David's ponytail was at least twelve inches longer than Richard Atkins's hair had ever been. The shade of David's hair was the only thing—besides his last name—that he had inherited from his father. Hannah told me once that Richard had been mysterious and a little dangerous when they'd first met; that had been her initial attraction. She had wanted to tame the bad boy in him, to reform him, until she realized he was perfectly happy being the way he was. Still, she'd been willing to stick with him, but the day Richard found out she was pregnant with David, he left town without saying a word.

"I asked you if it was raining," David repeated.

"What? No, of course not. There's not a cloud in the sky."

"Then why the umbrella?"

I'd honestly forgotten I was holding it. "Well, just because it's not raining now doesn't mean it won't later."

I hoped that statement made more sense to him than it did to me, but I wasn't about to admit that I'd been using it for protection.

"I guess," he said. "I came in early to clean up, but everything looks just like it did when I left it."

"You didn't think they'd leave the body here, did you? Looking for a chalk outline, perhaps?"

He was clearly appalled by my comment, and I realized it probably *had* sounded a little harsh. "Sorry, I guess I'm still a little on edge."

David smiled in relief. "Me, too, but I wasn't going to be the first one to admit it. Do they have any idea who might have done it?"

"Besides me, you mean? No, but I'm hoping our esteemed sheriff is out tracking down clues even as we speak."

I wasn't ready to open the shop yet, so David and I kept the door locked and the overhead lights off. We managed well enough with the sunlight coming in through the windows. I wasn't sure if we'd be deserted or jammed with customers today. It was hard to tell what was going to happen on a good day, and I had a feeling in my gut that this was going to be anything but one of those. I studied the laden shelves that covered the walls in the front half of the shop and checked our inventory of bisque-fired pieces, just in case we were busy today.

Most folks don't realize it, but to glaze a pot, it almost always takes two trips to the kiln. The first firing is the bisque stage. That hardens the clay into a porous ceramic and makes it easier to glaze in the next step. After the pieces are decorated with paints and then coated with glaze, they are fired again. The results are dramatic, going from dull, faded pieces to elegantly glazed and shiny pottery.

At Fire at Will, we offered mugs, salad plates, full-sized dinner plates, bowls, vases, and other items for our customers to decorate. At each of the four tables in the paint-your-own section, we had brushes, stencils, and sponges, along with a selection of glazes and paints from which customers could choose. The paints were all non-toxic, so they could eat and drink out of their wares once we'd fired them a second time. There was a long table for snacks, or it could double as a buffet if someone were having a birthday party, a wedding celebration, or some other catered event. In the back space we had three pottery wheels, four kilns, a bathroom, a small couch, a tiny office, and a storage area. It was a business I'd always dreamed of owning, and though it took a great deal of hard work to keep it afloat, Fire at Will was a labor of love for me.

As we checked our inventory levels, David asked me suddenly, "You don't have much faith in Sheriff Hodges, do you?"

I shook my head. "He's hanging on to his job until he can retire with full benefits. I doubt he'd recognize a clue if it snuck up and bit him on the nose."

David nodded. "I thought you'd probably say that. You know what that means, don't you?"

"That the killer will probably never be caught?" I asked.

"Not unless we find him ourselves."

I frowned, then asked, "How do you know it's a 'he'?"

"Hey, I believe in girl power as much as the next guy. Okay, let's go find her, then."

"David, what makes you think we can solve this ourselves? I'm a pottery-shop owner and you're my assistant. We're qualified for raku firing, not police work."

"We can get help, then," he said enthusiastically. "You've got lots of connections."

"You can't be serious."

He nodded. "Just hear me out. We can start with the Firing Squad. Jenna Blake is a retired judge; that means she's got to still have friends in the legal world. Sandy Crenshaw is a reference librarian, so I doubt there's a topic she can't research."

"Enough. This is foolishness."

"Is it?" David asked. "Butch Hardcastle could help, too. You know he could."

Butch was a retired and reformed crook, a big and burly man who loved decorating porcelain figurines. "I suppose you think Martha could help, too."

"Are you kidding me? She knows everybody in town. I'm telling you, we can do this."

"All we *need* to do is check on the firing from last night," I said. "I don't want to hear any more nonsense about us solving this ourselves. Agreed?"

"Fine," David said reluctantly.

I was restocking the cash-register till with money when David came back up front. I didn't like the look on his face.

"What's wrong?"

"You turned the kilns on yesterday evening, didn't you?"

"Yes, of course." I'd had to admit to the sheriff that I hadn't been sure, but I wasn't about to tell David.

"That's funny."

"What?"

"It's nothing. The firing should be done by now, but the witness cones are still upright. Something must be wrong with the kilns."

The best way to tell if a firing is done is when premade test cones of clay droop in the heat of the kiln at the proper temperature. In theory, a perfect firing would see the cones bent over at ninety degrees, so they should have been sagging like a dowager's chin by now. "Wonderful. That's just what we need, another expensive repair bill."

"Maybe it's just a fluke," David said.

"Maybe," I agreed. I glanced at the clock and saw that it was 10 A.M., time to open for the day. Taking a deep breath, I asked David, "Are you ready?"

"We might as well open up. I just hope we don't get mobbed with customers looking for information about the murder."

I wasn't sure what I'd been expecting, but as I unlocked the door and opened it, we were greeted by nothing but a chilly breeze. I poked my head out and saw people milling up and down the walkway, though none were heading in our direction.

"It looks like it's going to be a quiet day," I said as I came back in. "They might not think we're open for business today because of what happened." I couldn't bring myself to say "murder." "Let's drag the sale table out front and see if it helps." We had a table of discounted pottery items that had flaws of one sort or another, or had been abandoned by their owners. Usually it was a sure way to get browsers to stop by, but after two hours without a single visitor, I was beginning to wonder if I should have bothered opening up after all.

I looked over and saw David smiling ruefully at me. Without waiting for him to speak, I said, "No. I'm not going to do it."

"What? I didn't say a word."

"But I know what you're thinking."

His grin didn't waver. "Then maybe you should open up a psychic's shop instead. Do you mind if I go ahead and take my lunch break?"

"I think I can handle the rush on my own," I said.

Ten minutes after David was gone, Herman Meadows, my landlord, poked his head in the shop. "I got here as fast as I could. What happened last night, Carolyn?" Herman was in his midfifties, a bantam of a man barely managing five and a half feet tall. I wasn't that fond of his choices of cologne, but he was a decent sort, at least to me. He apparently thought of himself as some sort of ladies man, but he'd never made a pass at me. I didn't know whether to feel virtuous about it or be offended by his lack of attention.

"Betty Wickline was murdered," I said.

"I heard that much," he said dismissively. "Did you do it?"

"You're so smooth, Herman. You should be on the police force. Of course I didn't."

He raised one eyebrow. "But if you did, you wouldn't exactly confess it to me, would you?" I didn't like the way he was grilling me, but at least he had the decency to express his doubts about my innocence to my face. That was more than I could say for some of my fellow townsfolk.

"You've got a point. What else would you like to know?"

"I'm wondering what she was doing here in the first place after hours. You didn't let her in, did you?"

"Don't be foolish. I'm not sure how she got into the shop. The sheriff asked me to make a list of everyone who has keys to the place."

He scowled. "Did you tell him that you probably left the door unlocked yourself? It's happened before, Carolyn. No matter how many times I've told you to be careful about locking up whenever you leave, sometimes you forget. I've jiggled your front doorknob more than once when I'm on my rounds inspecting my properties, and it's opened to my touch without a key more times than I can count."

That was all the lecturing I was going to take from him. "It happened twice in the last six months. Sometimes I slip. But it was locked last night when I left. I'm certain of it."

"How can you be so positive? For that matter, you could have used your key this morning to unlock a door that was already open."

"That's impossible."

"I don't know why."

I smiled at him, then said, "Because I didn't unlock the door this morning at all. David was already here."

He shook his head in obvious disgust. "You should tell the sheriff about leaving the place unlocked before, Carolyn. He needs to know."

"I will if he asks," I said. "Is that all? I've got work to do."

He looked around the shop's deserted aisles. In a gentler voice, he said, "I'm sorry business is off. Don't worry, they'll come back. Give them some time."

At least he didn't make any cracks about me meeting my rent payment. Herman wasn't a bad guy, he just sort of focused on the bottom line. "Thanks," I said as I started tidying up the area around the register.

"If you need me, give me a call," he said. "Now I've got to check on my other properties." Herman owned and managed several of the shops along the brook, having inherited them from a grandfather who'd seen the great potential of converting the walkway into a tourist attraction.

I was still tidying up the register display area when the front door chimed.

"Oh, it's just you," I said as my husband walked in.

"I can leave, if you'd like," Bill said gruffly. How is it that men look so majestic when they age, and I just seem to look older? His hair was a lion's mane of silver, and though he'd gained a few pounds over the years, he still might be able to fit into the suit he'd worn at our wedding, whereas I'd have to have some serious alterations—to my body or my gown—to get my wedding dress over my hips ever again.

"Stay, you old goof."

He looked around the deserted shop. "Kind of quiet in here."

"You could hear a cricket's thoughts," I said.

"Has it been like this all day?"

"No, this is the highlight. At least you came."

Bill stroked his chin. "I was afraid of that. What are you going to do about it?"

"David thinks we should solve the murder ourselves."

Before I had a chance to tell him I thought the idea was sheer nonsense, Bill said, "You'll do no such thing."

"Is that an order?" I felt the hair on the back of my neck stiffen.

"Call it what you want. I'm just telling you not to do it, Carolyn."

"Bill Emerson, I thought by now you'd have learned that you're not in charge of me. I'll do whatever I see fit."

He glared at me a second, then said, "You're a stubborn woman, you know that, don't you?"

"I take that as a compliment. After all, I learned from the best."

He shook his head, then said, "Just be careful. Don't do anything foolish, and don't take any chances."

"Don't you have a dresser to make?" Now that the old fool had backed me into a corner, I had no choice but to try to figure out who had murdered Betty Wickline, so I might as well get started. There was no way on earth I was going to admit to my dear husband that I'd had no intention of getting involved until he'd prodded me into it, and I surely couldn't back down now.

"I've got two of them to do, as a matter of fact. Thought I might take you to lunch," he grumbled. "What do you say?"

It was a sweet thought, but I wasn't all that receptive at the moment. "I can't. I'm busy."

"Doing what?" he asked.

He had a point. I could have left the front door standing wide open and no one would have stepped inside. "I've got to solve this murder."

"Fool woman," I heard him mutter under his breath.

"What does that make you? You married me."

He startled me by hugging me close to him. "I don't want anything to happen to you."

Honestly, sometimes he could be so sweet. "Don't worry. I'll be careful."

"You'd better be," he said. "I've gotten used to having you around."

I broke from his grip and shooed him out. "Go on, I've got work to do."

After Bill was gone, I thought about how to go about investigating Betty's murder. David would be delighted—he was a man of action at heart—but I wasn't about to just charge into an investigation. I needed some advice.

It was time to call in the reinforcements, and that meant the Firing Squad.

Chapter 2

"Thanks for coming, everyone. I really appreciate it," I said as I addressed the members of the Firing Squad later that evening after I'd closed the shop for the night. "I need your help."

"Somebody you need handled?" Butch Hardcastle asked. He had the body of a lumberjack, and a pair of big, beefy hands that had seen some mayhem over the years. I was certain that the man was no stranger to violence in his past, no matter how much he professed to the world that he had reformed.

"It's not that kind of problem," I said. "I need to solve Betty Wickline's murder, or I might lose the business. We didn't have a single customer today, and while I've got a bit of a financial cushion set aside for emergencies, I can't afford many more days like the one I just had." Another reason, one I wasn't all that eager to share with the group, was that I wanted to solve the murder so I could show my dear husband I was perfectly capable of doing it, no matter what it took.

"I was tied up with the kids or I would have come by this afternoon," said Martha apologetically. You'd never know by looking at her that she had five children. When I'd been pregnant with my first son, I'd gained twenty-five pounds that still refused my efforts to vanquish them, but Martha was as willowy as a sapling.

Sandy Crenshaw said, "I had to work all day myself. We had six field trips visit the library and I had to give the same spiel six times in a row. It's a wonder I can talk at all." Sandy was a cute and curvy brunette with dazzling brown eyes and a ready smile.

Jenna Blake said sternly, "Carolyn, I want my objections on record. You shouldn't try to take the law into your own hands."

"She has to, if the sheriff isn't going to do anything," Butch said. For some odd reason, he and Jenna had formed a warm friendship that sometimes bordered on flirtatious, despite their divergent histories on opposite sides of the law.

"Butch," Jenna said with some affection, "Hodges may be getting on in years, but that doesn't mean he's not competent."

"It doesn't mean he is, either. Whose side are you on, anyway?"

"Carolyn's, and you know it."

"That's good, because the way you were talking, I wasn't sure there for a second."

Martha spoke up. "Carolyn, I'm sure we'd all love to help, but what can we do?"

David piped up, "That's why we need all of you," then he stopped abruptly as he glanced over at me. "Sorry, this is your show." I was amazed he'd been able to hold his tongue as long as he had. My assistant was cutting class to be at the meeting tonight, something I knew his mother would strongly disapprove of if she was ever made aware of it, but I hadn't had the heart to tell him he couldn't stay. After all, Fire at Will was a part of his life, too, and if it was in danger of closing, he had just as much a right to be there to defend it as anyone else.

I nodded, then continued. "We need information about Betty Wickline before we can take any action in finding her killer. Could you all ask around, do some quiet digging, and see what you come up with? If you get anything, call me here and let me know what you find. It's important that you each realize that I don't want to get any of you directly involved in this in case there's trouble later, but I need information, and you're the best sources I've got."

"Like I said, I'd be glad to put a little pressure on anybody you need. Just say the word and drop a name, and it's as good as done," Butch said.

Jenna patted his hand. "You'll do no such thing. We'll approach this on the proper side of the law. You're reformed now, remember?"

He grinned at her. "I know, but I could have a relapse, especially if it might help Carolyn's situation."

"Honestly, I just need you all to snoop around a little. Nobody should lean on anybody, okay? That's it. That's why I asked you all here."

Martha looked at the clock, a salt-glazed piece reminiscent of Salvador Dali's melted timepieces. "I've got a sitter until nine. Is there any reason we can't have a little fun while we're here?"

"No reason in the world," I said, suddenly glad for the distraction. After all, I'd opened Fire at Will for just that reason, to share my passion for clay with the world. It was time, if only for an hour or two, to forget all about Betty

Wickline and focus on what had brought us all together in
the first place.

David's cell phone rang, and from the troubled look on
his face, I didn't need more than one guess to tell me it was
Hannah. He said defensively, "I'm busy. No, I didn't go to
class tonight. Fine. All right. I'm going."

He slammed the cell phone shut, then said, "Sorry, I've
got to go."

"That's all right. We really are finished." I started walking with him toward the door when he said softly to me, "I
can let myself out."

After he was gone, Butch said, "You know something?
I want to start a new project."

"Not getting tired of porcelain figures, are you?" I
asked. Butch loved doing miniatures, and even with his
large hands, he had a delicate touch with a paintbrush.

"No, but I thought I might branch out a little. The other
day, you promised me you'd teach me to hand-build a
coiled pot, remember?"

"Ooh, that sounds like fun," Jenna said.

Martha smiled. "If it's okay with you and Sandy, would
you mind teaching us all how to do it?"

Sandy glanced at her watch, then said, "I'd love to stay,
but I've got a date. I told him if we finished up early we
could still go out to dinner."

I smiled. "You need to scoot, then."

She looked at the table where we'd be working. "I don't
know. This sounds like fun; maybe Jake will give me a rain
check."

"Or maybe he won't," Martha said.

"If he doesn't, he's nuts," Butch said.

"Why, aren't you sweet." Sandy leaned over and kissed
his cheek. Though Butch was a big man, and there was no

doubt in my mind he must have been a rough customer when he was a crook, he blushed from the kiss.

"I didn't mean anything by it," he said as he wiped Sandy's lipstick from his cheek.

"You didn't mean what you just said?" Sandy asked innocently, trying to hide her laughter.

"I . . . you know . . . I just . . ."

Jenna said, "Stop torturing him."

"But it's so much fun," Sandy said as she headed for the door.

I followed her and called out to the others, "I'll be back in a second."

"You don't have to walk me to the door," Sandy said. "I know the way."

"I've got to lock the place up behind you." The last thing in the world I wanted was for somebody to stumble in on us, especially while I was planning to circumvent a police investigation, and like it or not, that was exactly what I was about to do.

"Sorry, I didn't think about that. Of course David would have his own key."

I undid the dead bolt and pulled the door open, but Sandy didn't go out right away. "I should have something for you tomorrow," she said.

"I don't want your work to suffer." I was beginning to regret the decision to bring the Firing Squad in on my investigation. At the moment, I was the only one directly involved in Betty Wickline's death. Well, not really involved. Not in the murder, anyway.

"Are you kidding? This is the most exciting thing that's happened to me in ages. I'm willing to bet if I snoop around long enough, I'll be able to come up with something on Betty."

"Just don't take any chances," I said.

Sandy laughed. "Nobody will know it's me. The Internet is the great new faceless society. I promise, not a soul will have any idea who's asking the questions. I know how to cover my tracks on the Web."

Her enthusiasm was infectious. "Have a nice date, then," I said.

"Oh, I will. Jake's a good guy, but it's not like he's my Mr. Right, or even Mr. Right Now. He's fun—we laugh when we're together—and for the moment, that's all I'm looking for."

After she was gone, I headed back to the workshop area of my store. I could handle up to twenty-four adults at the six tables up front in the paint-your-own-pottery section, or fifty children, which was more than I really liked to have in the place at one time, even with David's help. I tried to offer a diverse selection of more than just the standard fare of plates, cups, bowls, and saucers. David was always coming up with new shapes and designs, sometimes with mixed results. While his enthusiasm could be charming at times, some of the things he'd thrown or hand-built would sit there and gather dust until long after I was gone.

There was a lot of potential activity crammed into my small shop space, and I made every inch of it count.

Butch, Martha, and Jenna were waiting impatiently for me at the large table in back, eager to get going.

"Sorry I took so long," I said. "I appreciate you all waiting." I walked over to the broken old refrigerator where I kept my clay. The material had to be stored in an airtight place, and a discarded fridge was the perfect solution, since I needed the clay to be kept from the air, not chilled.

"We didn't have much choice," Butch said. "I wanted to get started, but Jenna insisted we wait for you. I've read a few things about it already, you know," he said proudly.

Jenna patted his arm lightly. "I know that, Butch, but we all want to learn this together."

I opened the fridge, unwrapped a slab of clay, then cut off a hefty chunk, enough for the four of us. After I divided it with a cutting wire into four roughly equal portions, I gave each potter a block and kept a roughly shaped cube for myself.

"Now let's knead the clay," I said as I leaned into the brown doughlike substance. "We've got to get the lumps out, and the air bubbles, too." It was much like kneading bread, something I'd enjoyed from the first time my hands hit the clay.

After everyone had kneaded their clay to a smooth consistency, I said, "First I'll show you how I do it, then you can try it yourselves. Take a large wooden dowel and roll out your clay until it's about a quarter- to a half-inch thick. You can use cheaters if you'd like."

I demonstrated by putting two half-inch slabs of wood on either side of my clay. Then, with a practiced motion, I gently rolled the clay out until both sides of my improvised rolling pin touched the wood.

Once I was satisfied with the thickness, I said, "Cut out a section for your base and set it aside. Then take the knife and cut ropes from the rest of your clay. Next, cut out a circle for your base piece. That's the bottom of your pot, so you need to put it on a turning platform to make it easier to work with."

"That's just like our lazy Susan, at home," Martha said.

"We have one, too. Next, take one of the ropes you cut and roll it with your hands out on the canvas tablecloth to make it into a snake. You don't have to wet the base with slip for the next step, but you can. Coil the snake you've made on top of the perimeter of the circle and work your way up in a spiral. When you run out of one coil, grab another piece and keep going until you're at the height you want. I think six inches is a good start."

"It looks like a snake charmer's basket," Butch said as he studied the result of his work. "I wanted smooth sides."

"We'll take care of that next," I said as I grabbed a hardwood modeling tool that was really nothing more than a round stick with a softened edge. I smoothed the inner wall by using the tool inside the pot and light pressure from my hand on the outside. All it took was a little carefully applied force. After that, I reversed the process, and I had a nice looking pot instead of the stacked coils of clay.

"Is that it?" Jenna asked. "Somehow, I thought it would be more difficult to do."

As I refined the outside even more with a rubber rib, I said, "It's not as easy as it looks, but I'm sure you'll all get the hang of it in no time."

As they each worked on their own pots, I offered suggestions when they were needed. Soon enough, my crew each had a pot ready for the first firing.

"Can we each do another?" Jenna asked. "That was quite enjoyable."

I glanced at the clock. "Sorry, but it's getting late, and I've got a big day ahead of me tomorrow. I'll fire these soon, and you can glaze them at our next meeting."

They helped me clean up as they always did—something I loved about the Firing Squad—and in no time the place was ready for tomorrow. I put our hand-built pots into one of the kilns, along with some other pieces I wanted to fire, set the temperature, and locked up the store. I suddenly regretted leaving the Intrigue in the upper parking lot on the other side of our downtown, since it was now quite dark out. I tried not to run as I rushed back to my car.

Was someone in the shadows watching me? I glanced back over my shoulder, but I couldn't see anyone. Honestly, I'd raised two sons and ran a semisuccessful business, but now I was dodging shadows. Finding Betty's body must have been harder on me than I'd realized, if it was making me this jumpy. Or was I being paranoid? It *was* possible, I had to admit, that someone might really be lurking in the shadows watching me. But the real question was, were they there to protect me, or was it something much more ominous? This was ridiculous. I was a grown woman, and now suddenly I was afraid of the dark?

"Is someone there? You might as well come out. I see you standing in the shadows."

I saw a figure move in the darkness as I groped in my purse for my pepper spray. From now on, I promised myself, I was either going to carry that umbrella from the shop or start wearing running shoes at night. There was no way on earth I could make a getaway in the shoes I was wearing; my only option would be to kick them off and try running across the pavers in my socks.

"Enough of this foolishness. Come out, I said." I tried to make my voice as harsh as I could, but there was more than a little quiver in it. Should I abandon my shoes and try to run anyway?

As the figure approached—at my insane bidding, no less—I braced myself for an attack. Perhaps my chances of defending myself were no better than Betty Wickline's had been, but I'd surely make my attacker rue the day he came after me.

I nearly collapsed when I saw the figure step out into the light. It was my husband. "Bill Emerson, what are you trying to do, give me a heart attack?"

"I didn't want you walking to your car in the dark by yourself," he said.

"Then why on earth didn't you come to the shop and announce yourself instead of hiding in the shadows like some

kind of mad fiend?" Honestly, the man could drive me
bonkers sometimes.

"Didn't think you'd like it if I just showed up like that,"
he said gruffly.

The poor dear, he was probably right. I don't respond
well to coddling; I never have. I kissed his cheek, something that clearly startled him, then said, "You have my
blessing to walk me to my car at night anytime you'd like."

"Good," he said. "Now let's get you home. I can't have
you out taking chances like this at night. Do you *want* to
be next?"

If only he knew to stop while he was ahead. There were
a dozen things I could have said in response, but for
tonight, I decided to let him have the last word. "Let's go
home."

He nodded, and I put my arm in his as he walked me to
my Intrigue. My husband, no matter how bristly he could
be at times, was quite a lovely man.

"Carolyn, you're so brave carrying on like you are doing.
What with all the talk around town." Kendra Williams—
owner of Hattie's Attic and the biggest gossip in Vermont—
had cornered me on the sidewalk the next morning before
I even made it to my shop. I'd parked in the upper lot
again, out of habit instead of having any legitimate reason
this time. I was more than a little grumpy before Kendra
even spoke.

Hannah had begged off on our morning coffee, and I'd
gone without myself. Blast it all, I needed that jolt to get
my day started, and quite frankly, I loved having a few
minutes with Hannah in the morning, too. But she'd
claimed she was buried up to her eyebrows in essays on
Shakespearean comedies and couldn't meet me. I didn't

believe her, not for one second. Hannah had been angry when she'd found David at the shop instead of at the university, and she was clearly taking it out on me. I'd have to make things right with her, and soon, even if it meant banishing David to an education he only tepidly embraced.

Now I had the owner of Hattie's Attic on my back, too. "Kendra, you need to believe me when I tell you that I didn't kill Betty Wickline."

She actually managed to look shocked by my abrupt declaration. "Carolyn, I never thought you did. I just meant that some of the tongues around here are wagging about what might have happened to poor Betty."

"Let them wag. I have to go."

Kendra called out to my rapidly departing back, "Call me if you need to chat. I'm here for you."

"Thanks, but I'd rather eat a turkey, raw," I said softly. I thought the woman wouldn't be able to hear me, but she must have had the ears of a basset hound.

"What did you say?" she called out sharply.

"I said thanks for the offer. I might just give you a call."

She didn't believe me—the arch of her eyebrows was clear about that—but she waved and said, "Please do."

"When pigs fly," I whispered, but just in case the old bat really could hear me, I added, "I said I'll try."

I'd have to watch what I said around the woman, no matter what the distance was. The last thing on earth I wanted was for Kendra Williams to have it in for me. As my key neared the lock of the door to Fire at Will, my hand actually shook. What was I going to find there today? Carolyn, I said softly to myself, you're acting foolish. You're a grown woman, a success in marriage and business. Go in the shop. Now.

I didn't quite believe the pep talk I'd just given myself, and for a moment, I wished Bill was there with me. There was no danger of that, though, not after the scolding I'd ended up giving him after all. My, how brave and independent I'd been in the safety of my own kitchen.

How cowardly I felt right now, though.

"Hello? David?" I called out as I walked into the shop.

On the minus side, my assistant wasn't there yet, though he'd been scheduled to come in early today.

On the plus side, there weren't any new bodies left scattered around the place.

I checked the store's answering machine, and found a "2" on it. The first message was from a woman in Burlington asking about discounted glaze, and the second was from David.

"Hey, Carolyn. Listen, I'm sorry, I know you were counting on me, but I'm not going to be able to make it in today. I've got to catch up on the work I missed last night. I'll talk to you soon." The poor boy sounded angry and cowed at the same time.

I picked up the phone and dialed Hannah's number at the university. I had a sneaking suspicion that if I called her cell phone, she wouldn't pick up.

"Hello, Professor Atkins."

"Hi, Hannah, I know you're busy, but I need a minute."

"You've got just that," she said curtly.

"Then let me come right out with it and say that I'm sorry. I wasn't trying to interfere with David's education. I know how important it is to you."

Hannah snapped, "It's important to him, too, you know. After he gets his degree, I don't care what he does with his life, but until he does, he's got to go to classes. You can't let him skip any more lectures, Carolyn."

"Wait a second. I can't make him go to class any more than you can." I'd already raised two boys, and I wasn't about to take David on as a surrogate third.

"You know what I mean."

I took a deep breath before I trusted myself to speak. I was on dodgy ground here, torn between my responsibilities to my friend and those to my employee. Being in the middle of a fight was not where I wanted to be. "I won't keep him here at the shop late," I said, "but he wants to be here in the day. Don't take Fire at Will away from him, or he might drop out of school altogether."

I heard a sharp intake of breath and then dead silence. I wondered for a second if I'd killed her. "Hannah? Are you still there?"

"I am, but I've really got to go."

"Blast it all, I really am trying to apologize." Hannah could be more stubborn than Bill sometimes, and that was saying something.

"I know. It's fine. We're all right, but I really do need to go. I'll call you later."

"Bye," I said as she hung up.

Had I made it better with that last comment, or perhaps worse? David's employment at my shop was a sore point with Hannah, but we couldn't keep tiptoeing around it. He wanted to be a potter, and he found something working for me that was lacking for him at school. There was no doubt that David had a gift for clay, but what he lacked was the discipline, the patience of a master potter. As for his attendance record in school, they'd have to work it out between themselves. I had a shop to run. I glanced at the schedule to see if we had any groups coming in, and breathed a sigh of relief when I saw that we were clear of group lessons. In a moment of temporary insanity, I'd offered the teachers of Maple Ridge Elementary an overly generous discount, and most of them had taken me up on it. Things were just starting to slow down again, and I was looking forward to a quiet day—despite my worry about the lack of business.

Twenty minutes after I opened the shop, I heard what sounded like a flock of grackles outside my door. When I peeked outside, I saw twenty-five or thirty grade-schoolers heading my way, led by a young blonde with a look of sheer exasperation on her face. I knew I had to stop the horde from pillaging my place, so I walked outside, putting myself between them and Fire at Will.

Before I could say a word, the woman leading them said, "Hi, I know I didn't call ahead, but I promised them a field trip, and the bowling alley isn't open, even though I called them yesterday, and one of the children threw up on the school bus and our parent chaperone Mrs. Beasley had to take her back to school, so I've got all these kids and I can't bear to disappoint them. I'm Emma Blackshire. I'm new."

I don't know how she managed to get all that out without taking a breath or a break, but she did. There was no way I could handle this crowd without help, and there were no reinforcements I could call on. I was about to turn her away when I spied one of the little boys, a towhead who looked just like my son Timothy when he was that age. The poor sweet child looked as though he were ready to burst into tears, and my heart melted.

"Bring them in," I said, and the young boy smiled. I was going to picture that expression all day. It was the only thing that was going to get me through what I knew was about to happen.

That, or a shot of bourbon, though I doubted Miss Blackshire would approve. Then again, based on her agitated state, she might just join me.

I managed to round up enough of the small bisque fired saucers we used for school groups, and the kids seemed to have a good time, though they did wreck the place as only a class of grade-schoolers could. After they were gone, I stacked two of the kilns and started firing their works. Once that was done, I was scrubbing down the tables when the front door opened. Not another student group, I prayed under my breath.

The second I saw who it was, I found myself wishing for the entire student body of the elementary school instead.

It was the sheriff, John Hodges, and I could see by the way he was looking at me this wasn't going to be pleasant conversation for either one of us.

"Come to paint some pottery, Sheriff?" I asked in the sweetest voice I could muster. If he could tell I was being sarcastic, he didn't show it.

"You're kidding, right?" he said. "I'm here about Betty Wickline."

"Give me a second. I need to turn off the lights and lock the door."

That stumped him. "What are you talking about, Carolyn?"

"I assume you've decided to dispense with an actual investigation and go ahead and arrest me. David's not coming in today, and I'd rather not leave the shop door standing wide open while you haul me off in the back of your squad car."

That made him mad—probably not the best tack I could have taken, but I resented even being on his suspect list. Honestly, I was probably the only one on it, knowing the sheriff's dislike for actual work.

"I'm not here to arrest you," he shouted.

"There's no need to yell. I can hear perfectly fine. If you aren't going to handcuff me, then why are you here?"

"Just because I'm not planning to arrest you this second doesn't mean I don't want to talk to you about what happened here. I need that list of people who have keys to your shop."

I'd nearly forgotten all about it. "It's in my purse. Let me get it." Still smarting from his tone of voice, I handed him my purse. "You'd better retrieve it yourself. You never know, I might have a gun stashed in there somewhere."

He looked at the offered purse like it was a snake. "I'm not fool enough to go diving into a woman's purse without more reason than you've given me. At least not yet."

I retrieved the list, with no more names added to it than I'd shared with Hannah, and handed it to him.

He studied it a second, then said, "I'll look into this."

"There's something else you should know," I added reluctantly.

"Well, don't make me pull it out of you. What is it?"

"There's a chance that I might have left the front door unlocked when I left the day of the murder. It's happened a few times before. Anyway, I thought you should know."

"And you're telling me this now?" He glanced down at the list. "That makes this pretty much worthless, doesn't it?"

"I'm not saying that I *did* leave the door unlocked. I just thought you should know it was a possibility. Oh, there's something else I should probably tell you. Robert Owens is on your list, and he's been out of town since before the murder. He went back to North Carolina three days ago to get the rest of his stuff. He's just moved to Maple Ridge."

"I'll check him out. Since I'm already here, I'd like to ask you a few more questions, if you don't mind." I hated orders that sounded like requests.

"Do I have any choice?"

"Don't be that way, Carolyn."

"Fine, ask away."

He looked at me a second before he proceeded.

"There's no easy way to ask this. When was the last time you saw Betty alive?"

"I told you that the night I found her body."

"Tell me again." His gaze never left me.

"She came into the shop that afternoon. We talked for a few minutes, then she left."

He raised one eyebrow. "What did you talk about?"

"Who remembers? It wasn't all that significant. Something about a firing, I think."

"Are you sure you weren't having an argument?" He was being much too smug for my tastes.

"Why? What have you heard?"

The sheriff shrugged. "I understand it wasn't so much of a conversation as it was a fight."

That was all I could take. "Where did you hear that? Tell me who it was."

He backed up a step. "It was an anonymous tip, but the whispered voice sounded like she knew what she was talking about."

"Then your heroic witness is full of hot air. Nobody was in the shop when Betty was here. Not even David."

Hodges looked at me a long time before he spoke. "Just because you say it, that doesn't make it so."

"Nor should you take the word of some coward with a telephone over mine. We've known each other a long time, John. Do you honestly think I'm capable of murder?"

He took much too long to answer to suit my tastes. "You've always had a sharp tongue, Carolyn, and Betty managed to bring out the worst in folks. I can't rule anything out yet."

"Well, until you do, perhaps you should start looking for the real killer instead of wasting your time with me. Now if you're not going to lock me up, I suggest you leave so I can go about my shop's business."

He nodded and headed toward the door, but before he left, the sheriff turned to me and said, "You're not planning any trips out of Maple Ridge anytime soon, are you?"

"Why do you ask?" Did he honestly think I was capable of murder? Or that even if I was, I'd actually flee the area? Honestly, where would I go? I'd lived here all my life.

"I'd just rather have you around in case I come up with any more questions for you."

"I'll be here," I said. I couldn't believe the sheriff actually thought I'd had something to do with Betty's death. He'd known me forever. But if he could believe it, other people might, too. I was going to have to do something to clear my name. There was no way I'd be able to live in Maple Ridge with the whispers and the speculation. If Sheriff Hodges wasn't going to help me, I was going to have to do it myself.

Chapter 3

I was so rattled after the sheriff left that it took a good half hour for me to settle back down. I'd pick something up, then forget why I had it in my hands. It would have been nice to have David back, but after my conversation with Hannah, I wasn't sure if I'd ever see my assistant again. I could manage to run Fire at Will by myself, but it wouldn't be nearly as much fun, and I could kiss lunches out goodbye forever. My friend Shelly ran her own diner, appropriately named Shelly's Café, but I knew our relationship didn't extend to her bringing me my lunch every day.

I remembered to check the hand-built coiled pottery pots the Firing Squad had made the night before, and suddenly realized that I had forgotten all about the kilns' earlier erratic behavior. What would I find when I opened them? Everything appeared to be fine as I took out each of the pieces and examined them in turn. Maybe the night Betty had died had been a single glitch and not the start of something worse. At least something appeared to be going right for me.

Customers were pretty sparse the rest of the morning. Okay, that's not entirely true. There would have to have been at least one customer for me to be able to call it sparse, and I hadn't had anyone else come in after the school kids. When the door chimed later in the day, I nearly leapt forward, eager to have some company, any company at all.

It was Butch. He took in the deserted shop. "Kind of empty, isn't it?"

"You're here between lulls," I said.

"How long has the last lull been?" he asked.

I thought about lying to him, but Butch had been a crook long enough to spot my weak attempts at deception. "Pretty much since Betty died," I admitted reluctantly.

"Don't worry, Carolyn, we'll fix this. I've got some stuff on the woman that might help."

"Like what?" I asked. Sheriff Hodges had shaken me more than I was willing to admit. I needed to find the killer myself if he was going to focus solely on me.

"Her ex wasn't too keen on her, that's for sure. That guy was paying alimony out the wazoo."

"You didn't rough him up, did you?" The last thing I wanted was to get one of my favorite customers and a member of the Firing Squad in trouble.

He laughed at my suggestion. "Naw, not Larry. He wouldn't be worth the effort. I tracked him down at Twilly's Bar last night and bought him a few drinks. I swear, that's all that happened."

"Does he have an alibi for the night she was murdered?"

Butch looked a little sheepish as he admitted, "To tell you the truth, he got drunk too fast for me to ask him about that. That guy shouldn't go to bars if he can't hold his liquor better than he was managing when I left."

The telephone rang, and I reached for it. "Hang on one second," I told Butch before I answered, "Fire at Will."

"Carolyn, this is Sandy. Have you got a minute? I might have something for you."

"Hang on a second, Sandy." I covered the phone with my hand. "Butch, Sandy's on the line. Was there anything else?"

He shook his head. "No, not yet. Don't worry, though. I'll come up with something."

"Don't try too hard, if you know what I mean."

He chuckled. "Now that all depends on how reluctant the folks I talk to are about having a conversation with me. Don't you worry about me."

He wasn't the one I was worried about, but before I could add any more admonitions, Butch was gone.

"Sorry about that. I'm back," I told Sandy.

"That's fine. I've been doing some digging on the Internet and I've come up with a few things on Betty. Did you know she was getting a huge alimony check every month from her ex-husband? That might be enough of a motive for murder."

"Butch already told me that. But how did you find out so quickly?"

"Public records for our county are online. How about this, then? You know how Betty liked to flaunt her nice things around town?"

I knew it only too well. She always had to have the latest model car and wear all the newest fashions. Her superior attitude toward the rest of us commoners had been one of the things I'd disliked so much about her. "She could be too much to take sometimes, couldn't she?"

"Well, it turns out she wasn't nearly as well off as she

wanted everyone to think. Betty was living way beyond her income. All she had was alimony, and while it probably felt like gouging to her husband, she had to live entirely off of it, since she didn't have any other income. The thing is, she never seemed to be short on cash, and I can't find out where the rest of her money came from."

"Perhaps she inherited it," I said.

"No, I checked her parents' wills, and there wasn't much left after their funeral expenses were paid off."

"Now how on earth did you discover that?" It amazed me how much Sandy had been able to find out in such a short period of time without ever leaving the library.

"Please, it's simple if you know where to look. Wills are a matter of public record, and so are final dispositions. Give me something hard."

"So where was she getting her money?"

"I wish I could tell you," Sandy said. "From what I can see so far, I'm having a hard time believing it's from a legitimate source. At least not one I've been able to track down. Don't worry, though. I'll keep digging."

"I'm amazed how much you've been able to find out so far."

"Believe me, with the Internet, there aren't nearly as many secrets as there once were."

That was a scary thought, one I wasn't all that eager to contemplate.

I wondered if any of the rest of my crew would check in. No doubt Martha had her hands full with her lively brood, but I knew she'd have the best chance of uncovering something about Betty's life that might be useful. The Mommy network was amazing in our small town. Martha had connections, through her children, to the most diverse group of people. It might take her some time to come up with something, but if she did, I was sure it would be gold.

Jenna could help from the legal end of our impromptu investigation, but she had an ethical streak in her that might hinder her effectiveness in aiding me. Still, if Betty had ever been involved in the criminal justice system, Jenna would know it.

To my surprise and great delight, David walked into the shop a little after one. "Hey, stranger, I wasn't sure I'd see you today."

He looked sheepish. "Sorry about that. You know how Mom can get."

"Don't do that. You know I'm a big fan of your mother's."

He nodded. "I know. I swear, sometimes I think you two are ganging up on me."

"Would we do that?" I tried to keep the laughter out of my voice, but it was impossible.

He laughed right along with me.

A moment later, I asked, "So, was it a full pardon, are you out for good behavior, or are you going to be on parole for a while?"

"Mom made sure there was no doubt in my mind about it. It's parole. Definitely. If I miss another class, I won't be able to come in for a week."

"Then I sincerely hope you go to class."

He grinned. "Even if you have to drag me there yourself, huh?"

I refused to match his smile. "No, I'm not going to get involved. This is between your mother and you." Then I patted his shoulder. "But I will say it's good to have you back."

"Thanks. I've been gone less than a day, and I already feel like it's been a month." He glanced around the shop. "Has it been this quiet all day? Maybe I should have stayed away to save you from paying my salary."

"Things will never get that tight," I said, though if the current trend kept up, I wouldn't be able to promise that forever. We needed customers in Fire at Will, and not just for their money. The business was a living entity, and it needed to be fed on a regular basis with laughter and fun as well as dollars and cents.

He nodded. "Thanks, I appreciate that. Listen, if you want to take a late lunch, I've got this covered."

"That's the best offer I've had all day," I said as I took off my Fire at Will apron. It was fire-engine red; one of my customers had made it especially for me. I'd protested that it was too nice to get muddied with clay, and she'd responded by making me three more. Since the extent of my sewing skill was limited to an errant button replacement now and then, I'd gladly accepted them, then had waived her bill for the month. I'd been trying to get David to wear one, but he'd resisted my attempts so far, opting for a potter's brown apron instead. The only thing I envied about his apron was that it didn't show stains.

"I think I'll take a walk and grab a bite," I said. "Just let me wash up."

I left the shop, determined to enjoy as much as I could of the nice day. Though it was April, there was still a nice nip in the air. The weatherman had threatened us with snow showers later in the week, but at the moment, the temperature was hovering in the lower fifties. The majority of the skiers had left the nearby Green Mountains, and it was too soon for our summer tourists. While I missed the revenues the other seasons brought, I didn't miss the crowds. I decided to walk on the sidewalk by the brook, which turned out to be a mistake, something I knew the second I heard Kendra calling my name. The woman was getting to be an absolute pest, and it was time to set her straight.

• • •

"Carolyn, there's something you should know," Kendra said as I neared her shop. "The police have been here."

"Have you been selling fake antiques again?" I said, not caring about her wince.

"I told you, and everyone else who would listen, my supplier gave me a phony certificate of authenticity. I refunded that man's money, didn't I? What else could I do?"

"You could have been more careful about who you bought your store stock from."

I was about to say something else when she cut me off. "The police weren't here about me. They were asking questions about you. I thought you should know."

So the sheriff was serious about coming after me. I'd been hoping he had just been posturing until he stumbled across the real killer, but evidently that hope was for naught. "What did he want to know? More importantly, what did you tell him?" Knowing Kendra, I wouldn't have been surprised if she'd claimed to be a witness to the murder to get a little attention.

"I had to tell the truth, didn't I?" Now why did she suddenly look so guilty?

"What did you tell him?" I had maneuvered her around so that her back was toward the brook. I was in no mood for her foolishness today.

She must have seen it in my eyes. "I've said too much already." As she started back to her shop, I moved toward her, cutting off her retreat.

"Kendra, don't do this."

"You're scaring me," she whined. "Get out of my way."

I could see real fear in her eyes. I stepped to the side. "I'm sorry. I'm just so upset."

Kendra bolted past me into her antique shop. It wouldn't have surprised me at all if she locked the door behind her.

Wonderful. Now I'd harassed the gossip queen of Maple Ridge out on our brook walk, in broad daylight. How long would it take her to call Sheriff Hodges to file a complaint? Surely I'd be in his lockup by nightfall.

I wasn't much in the mood for lunch anymore, or to be around people, for that matter. I started back to Fire at Will and was surprised to see Jenna Blake approaching me.

"Carolyn, have you lost your mind?" she snapped at me.

"That's the question, isn't it? I'm guessing you saw what just happened."

"You mean you accosting Kendra Williams in broad daylight? The whole town probably saw it. You need to get control of that temper of yours."

"It wasn't what it looked like," I said in my defense. "Okay, maybe it was, but she deserved it. That woman has a way of driving me crazy."

"Like Betty Wickline did?"

I studied her dour expression. "Maybe Butch was right to question your loyalties. Whose side are you on?"

"You don't have to ask, you know that. But don't make things any harder on yourself than you have to."

I was in no mood to be lectured. "Thanks for the legal advice. Feel free to send me a bill."

I wasn't sure how she would react, but her laughter startled me. I asked, "What's so funny, Jenna?"

"You are determined to thumb your nose at the world right now, aren't you?"

I wasn't all that amused by her question. "I'm willing to admit that when I'm pushed, I have a tendency to push back."

"That's what I'm afraid of. I've got some information for you, but I'm not sure you're in any mood to receive it. Perhaps we'll talk later."

As she started to walk away, I said, "Wait a second. I'm sorry. Maybe my blood sugar's down. Do you have time to get something to eat? Something to go? We could go over to Shelly's."

I still didn't want to be around people, but Jenna was different. In an odd little way, the Firing Squad was a surrogate family for all of us. We'd helped each other through sickness, divorce, and other heartaches in the five years the club had been together. Even death. One of our charter members, Julie Price, had died in a car accident on her way to one of our regular meetings. I still kept the last pot she'd thrown in my office as a reminder that life is fleeting and that you have to grab every chance you get.

"Lunch sounds good, but I don't have time to go to Shelly's," Jenna said. "Why don't I grab something for us at In the Grounds? Would you like a coffee with your sandwich?"

"Better make it bottled water. I'm jumpy enough as it is without adding caffeine to the mix." I reached into my purse for some money, but Jenna said, "Don't worry about it. It's my treat."

I wasn't about to say no. I didn't want to offend her, and I knew Jenna could easily afford it.

I found a bench by the water, and she soon returned with our sandwiches.

"I appreciate you doing this," I said.

"It's my pleasure. I had to eat anyway," she added with a grin.

"I mean helping me with this impromptu investigation. I hate to get all of you involved in my problems."

"Your problems are ours. Remember what brought me to Fire at Will the first time?"

"I'm not likely to forget. You were a little lost."

Jenna laughed heartily. "That's a vast understatement,

and you know it. I was floundering. After Eric died and I took early retirement, I just about lost my reason for living. You and the Firing Squad helped me recapture it. You're all the family I really have now."

It all came back so vividly. Jenna had been widowed six years before, and her late husband had left her extremely well off. The law had lost its appeal with his demise, and she'd opted for early retirement from the bench. Jenna had walked into the shop searching for something a year later, and she'd apparently found it with our little group.

"That's just about the sweetest thing I've ever heard anyone say," I said.

"Then Bill's in trouble. He's not exactly a 'roses and poetry' kind of fellow, is he?"

"No, but I love him just the same." I took a bite of my sandwich, tacked on a sip of water, then said, "If you're ready to tell me your news, I'm fine now."

Jenna stared at the brook a minute before answering. "I hesitate to mention this, because it's really nothing more than a courthouse rumor. Still, it might give you some insight into Betty's killer, and I truly do want to help. It's just that I abhor gossip."

"Don't think of it that way, then. You're just sharing information."

"I suppose," she said thoughtfully. "Do you happen to know Tamra Gentry?"

"Who doesn't? I don't mean I know her personally, but I do know that she has more money than the bank, and she got away with murder, too, didn't she?" Rumor had it that Tamra Gentry was wealthy beyond all dreams of avarice. Unfortunately, she also had a penchant for nineteen-year-old men. That wasn't necessarily a problem when she was twenty, but she'd been fifty-seven when she'd chosen her last one, and he was a bad sort, at that. There were rumors that Tamra had tried and failed to fully hide unexplained bruises on her arms and face more than once before her latest paramour turned up murdered. The newspaper had tried and convicted her with their reporting of the homicide—discounting the apparent batterings—but a jury had deadlocked on the case. With no verdict one way or the other and no retrial likely because of the expense involved, Tamra had walked away a free woman.

"She wasn't convicted, but she wasn't found innocent, either. The problem is, I shouldn't know this, but one of the bailiffs at the courthouse accidentally overheard something he shouldn't have. Betty Wickline served as forewoman on that jury, and ironically enough, she had the one 'not guilty' vote of the twelve that locked them in a hopeless mess."

I could see Betty opposing the majority out of pure cussedness, and I didn't doubt she'd stepped into the forewoman's position by simply volunteering. I'd served on a few juries myself, and I'd even been talked into leading the jury room's discussions once. I hadn't served on a murder case, though. Mine had been an inflated charge of conveying threats, and it was so obvious who was lying and who was telling the truth, one witness would have made Pinocchio's nose proud.

"That doesn't necessarily mean anything, does it? You knew Betty. She could be as stubborn as anyone when it came to her opinion."

"That's not all. The bailiff—and I'm not going to tell you his name, so don't ask—saw something suspicious, though he could never prove it. After the jury was dismissed, he was in the parking lot sneaking a cigarette before the next case. He was behind some bushes, since he's not supposed to be seen smoking on the grounds, and he saw Tamra's attorney say something to Betty at her car."

"What could he have said?"

"My friend braced the attorney on it, but he claimed he was just warning her about a tire that was nearly flat. When Betty corroborated the story, there was nothing he could do about it, but he's wondered about it ever since."

"Is there any chance it was as innocent as they both claimed?"

Jenna raised an eyebrow. "Not likely. You might want to look into Betty's bank accounts, if there's any way you can manage that without a court order. I'd be interested to see if there were any large deposits made right after the case. Jury tampering is an ugly thing, but I know it happens."

"It's too late to prove it now, isn't it?"

"They might not be able to prosecute now that their star witness is dead, but I'd love to put some pressure on that lawyer, Joe McGrath. He argued a few cases before me, and I never trusted him." She finished her sandwich. "It might not be anything, but I thought you should know."

"Thanks. As a matter of fact, Sandy discovered that Betty was living way beyond her means. A little blackmail might just explain her inflated income."

Jenna shook her head. "I wonder if most people realize just how dangerous the Internet is in the hands of a skilled reference librarian."

"They probably wouldn't be able to sleep at night if they did," I said. I finished my sandwich as well. "Thanks for lunch, and for the information. I hope you didn't bend your ethics for me."

"I wouldn't do that, and you know it, but I'm willing to help any way I can."

"I appreciate that," I said.

I had some new information, and an increased respect and affection for Jenna. I knew how seriously she took the law, and she'd not only managed to refrain from lecturing me on letting the sheriff handle the investigation himself, but she'd also actively gone out in search of information to help me. It was wonderful having friends like her.

Back at the shop, David handed me a note on his way out the door for a quick bite of his own. I didn't even glance at it as I asked, "Were you busy while I was gone?"

He shook his head. "We might as well have locked up and gone together. The only thing I did was take that phone message. Well, that's not strictly true. I did clean up some in back, but we didn't have any customers. I'm sorry."

"It's not your fault, David. They'll come back. Just give them a little time." It was a fake batch of courage I was trying to sell. The drastic drop in business *was* worrying me. Did folks around town actually believe I could have had something to do with Betty's death? Why else would they stay away in droves? Or was it just a seasonal lull, one I normally embraced? Either way, I couldn't be sure.

After David was gone, I glanced at the note. It was from Martha. With five children—three of them still too young for school—I marveled that she had any time or energy for anything else, let alone snooping around for me.

I called her right back. "Hi, Martha, I just got your message."

"Hey, Carolyn. Could you give me a few minutes here? The twins are refusing to eat their lunch, and I'm about to give up and just let them go hungry." Martha was the most caring and nurturing soul I knew. She loved her children more than life itself, but even a saint's patience can wear thin on occasion.

"I'll be here for the rest of the afternoon," I said. "Call me back when you can."

In the background, I heard one of the twins shouting, "I won't. I won't. I won't." A second later, her fraternal twin chimed in, and Martha hung up without saying good-bye.

I'd always dreamed of having twins, but when the time came, I was thankful my boys came one at a time. I didn't know how she managed it.

I was refilling some of the squeeze bottles with glaze when the telephone rang. "Fire at Will," I said as I re-capped one.

"Sorry about that," Martha said, her voice much calmer than it had been before.

"Hey, you've got a lot going on there, no need to apologize," I said. "What's up?"

"I heard something kind of tawdry that might help you."

"Even if it doesn't, I'm always in the mood for tawdry. Where'd you pick up this juicy little item?"

"I was asking some innocent questions at Mommy Time. You wouldn't believe some of things I heard about Betty Wickline." Mommy Time was Maple Ridge's gathering place for the most diverse group of mothers, and some fathers, too. While they played together with their children, the parents covered topics from A to Z. I wished they would have had something like that when I was home alone raising the boys. Being a stay-at-home mom was the most isolating experience of my life, and while I loved my sons, I leapt for joy when my youngest went to preschool. There was no separation anxiety there. I was ready to get out in the world again.

"Tell me," I said.

"It seems Betty had a new man in her life. The other night, Ryan Glade was out jogging and found Betty in her car with the windows steamed up. Only she wasn't alone."

"She had a house of her own. Why on earth would she carry on like a teenager in a parked car?"

"I asked that myself," Martha said. "Apparently, Ryan mentioned spotting her the next day, and Betty panicked until she realized that Ryan hadn't seen her partner. That's when Betty hinted smugly that the man in question wouldn't want to be seen with her in public. The only reason I can think of is that he might be married to someone else. Do you think that could have some bearing on the case?"

"It's certainly worth looking into. Thanks, Martha, I appreciate this."

"Always glad to help." In the background, I heard a sudden burst of crying, coming through the telephone like it was in stereo. "I've got to go," she said abruptly.

"Is everything all right?" I asked.

"It's the twins. I don't see any blood, so at least that's something."

She hung up before I could get any more information out of her. I wouldn't have traded my life for Martha's if there were a million-dollar bonus attached.

I couldn't exactly wait on customers I didn't have, and I didn't feel like doing any pottery work myself, so I grabbed my sketch notebook from my office and turned to a fresh page. Maybe writing down my thoughts would help. So far, I'd found out that Betty had more money than she should have, had an ex who wanted her off his payroll, may have taken a bribe or was blackmailing the richest woman in our county, and was having an affair with a possibly very married man. The woman led a more active life in the last six months than I had in fifty-odd years.

The problem, as I saw it now, was to find out who in Maple Ridge *didn't* have a reason to kill Betty Wickline.

Chapter 4

"I can see you're just buried in work. Should I take the rest of the day off to save you some money?" David, back from his own late lunch, was earnest in his request, and for a second, I thought about taking him up on his offer. But then I suddenly had a better idea.

"Tell you what," I said. "Why don't you stay here and keep the shop open, and I'll see what I can come up with on Betty Wickline's murder?"

"Should you be doing that alone? We can lock the shop, and I'll come with you."

"I appreciate that, but I can't afford to lose the income, just in case someone comes by." That was true enough, but I also didn't want to have to explain to Hannah how I'd managed to drag her son into the murder investigation. I couldn't afford to lose my best friend over this. If it came to that, I'd rather lose my business.

He looked duly disappointed, so I had to throw him

some kind of bone. "Why don't you experiment with that new glaze you've been trying to develop?"

"Are you sure you don't mind?"

"Be my guest. Just remember, write down everything you do, and make small batches. Those custom glazes and pigments you're playing with can get expensive."

"I will. I promise." David had been trying for months to come up with a signature color for his work, a new shade or hue he could call his own. I understood Hannah's desire to see her only child get a degree in something he could use, but David was a born potter and glazer, and it would be a shame if those talents had to take a backseat to a career he didn't want. But, as I told myself a thousand times, I'd raised my boys, and I wasn't about to take on David as well. He and his mother were going to have to work it out between them without any interference from me. At least not much. Honestly, I was trying to stay out of it, but really, who can stand idly by when they see someone they care about making a mistake? No, I knew I could really muck things up, despite my good intentions, and if it had been January, I would have made it a New Year's resolution to butt out of their affairs. At least I was going to try.

Now I had a free afternoon to investigate. It was time to determine which of the leads the Firing Squad had given me might point me toward Betty Wickline's murderer.

As I walked around town, I ran into Herman Meadows coming out of Rose Colored Glasses. "Shouldn't you be working?" he said. "You didn't shut down the pottery shop, did you?"

"David's watching the store. Is this one of yours, too?" I asked as I gestured to the stained-glass shop.

"Sure is. I've got Hattie's Attic, this place, yours, and In the Grounds. That's just in this part of Vermont. I've also got some property in North Carolina."

"Did you inherit that as well?"

He drew himself up to his full five-and-a-half-foot height. "I'll have you know that I've done more with my life than just sit around collecting rent. I've got dreams, Carolyn, and I'm making them happen."

"Sorry, I didn't mean anything by it."

He frowned, then it abruptly turned into a grin. "That's okay. I guess I'm still a little touchy. My aunt called me up this morning and chewed me out. She said I wasn't ambitious enough, and I guess she kind of pushed my buttons. I didn't mean to take it out on you."

"I don't mind," I said.

"Well, I gotta go. I've got a ton of stuff to do today."

I wished I could say the same thing, but if I did, I'd be lying.

As far as the murder investigation was concerned, the afternoon was a total failure. I'd tried to strike up conversations with a dozen different folks I knew, but all I got for my trouble was a handful of rushed good-byes and a few outright snubs. Did these people actually think I could have killed Betty Wickline? Their reactions frustrated me on so many levels. I'd been born and raised in Maple Ridge, I'd raised two sons and owned my own business for years, yet I was being treated like an outcast. I wasn't used to being a pariah in my own hometown. Still, if anything, my new status only fueled my drive to find out who really had killed Betty.

Thoroughly disgusted with the folks I thought were my friends, I made my way back to Fire at Will. As I strolled along the brook walk, I suddenly realized I'd been ignoring my best source for gossip in all of Maple Ridge. If there was something going on in the shadows of our quaint old town, there was one woman who would surely know about it. It was time to brace Kendra Williams in her own little lion's den.

Hattie's Attic contained the most eclectic collection of goods for sale I'd ever seen in my life. There were some truly wonderful pieces buried in the aisles of chairs, signs, baskets, woodworking tools, and a myriad of other old things, but there were also some items of doubtful heritage and shady authenticity. The place was a little too dark for my tastes, its dim lighting reminding me of my grand-mother's parlor, and I couldn't imagine how Kendra spent so much time there. Then again, she probably wondered the same thing about me and all my messy glazes and clay.

I didn't see Kendra when I first walked into Hattie's Attic. Then I spotted a movement in back by the vintage clothing. Was she actually hiding from me?

"Kendra, come out here right now."

Her nose poked out of the racks. "What do you want, Carolyn? I've got a customer coming any second to pick up an armoire. He's bringing three of his friends to help him." The woman was absolutely cowering.

I started walking toward where she was hiding.

"I mean it," she shouted. "They'll be here any second."

"Then we don't have long, do we? Kendra, you know this town better than anyone alive. I need your help."

There was a ruffling sound in the clothes as she started to inch slowly forward. "What do you want to know?"

"Was Betty Wickline seeing anyone? I'm interested in a married man in particular."

I saw a brief flash of a smile from Kendra, and I knew I had her. Even if she believed in her heart that I'd killed Betty, her desire to spread gossip was greater than her need for personal safety. "Why do you want to know?" she asked as she stepped free of the racks.

"Because I have to find out who killed Betty before I go broke. Nobody's coming to my shop, and half the town won't even speak to me."

"So you're going to try to find the killer on your own?" She sounded incredulous.

"I am, with a little help from my friends." I choked back a breath as I added, "Like you."

She approached me and held my shoulders with both hands. "Carolyn, I never doubted you. You can count on me."

I think I liked her better when she was cowering in the clothes. "So, have you heard anything?"

"There have been rumors for the last few weeks, but I haven't been able to pin anything down."

"That's too bad," I said. If Kendra didn't know, I had no idea how I was going to find out.

"Don't give up that easily. I never had a reason to push for the information until now. Give me until noon tomorrow and I'll have an answer for you. I'm so glad you came to me, Carolyn."

I had to get out of there, and the stale smell of the place wasn't the only reason. "Let me know as soon as you can, okay?"

"I will. You can count on me," she said again.

I left, fighting the urge to run back to my shop. There was someone else I could talk to, but it would take the guts of a con man to do it. If I could speak with Tamra Gentry, I might be able to discover if she had a reason to want Betty Wickline dead.

•   •   •

Tamra's mansion sat on the ridge full of maples our town had been named for. It was almost as if she was looking down on the rest of us from her lofty aerie. Lovely maples dotted the hillside, and in the autumn, their blazing leaves made the mountain look as though it were on fire. Her house was grand, a three-story colonial with massive white columns in front. I rang the bell, suddenly a little nervous about the way I was dressed. While my slacks, blouse, and jacket were good enough for everyday life, I felt more than a little underdressed at the moment.

To my surprise, an actual butler answered the door, and he managed to register his disdain for my interruption with nothing more than the slightest movement of his upper lip. "Yes?" he said, making the word sound more like an invocation than a query.

"I'd like to see Mrs. Gentry, please."

"Is she expecting you?"

"No," I said. I had to have some reason for calling on her, I mean, other than the real one. I said the first thing that came into my mind. "I'm here fundraising for the elementary school."

"I'm sorry, but Mrs. Gentry is indisposed. Perhaps if you'd call later for an appointment."

He was just closing the door when I heard Tamra's voice. "James, who is it?"

Before he could answer, she brushed past him. I'd met Tamra a few times in the past, but our social circles didn't exactly coincide. She was a striking woman, even without the cosmetic surgery. Her hair was like spun platinum, and her carriage was haughtily erect. I only hoped I'd look half that good when I was her age.

"I know you," she said lightly. "You run that quaint little shop in the village."

"Fire at Will," I admitted.

"What a delightful name. Well, don't just stand there. Come in. James, we'll have coffee in the parlor. Unless you'd prefer tea," she said, looking at me. "I have some wonderful blends."

"Coffee's fine," I said.

"Wonderful. Come now, don't tarry."

I followed her into the living room, trying to take in all of the real antiques along the way. Despite the evidence to the contrary about her choice in men, in other things, Tamra Gentry had excellent taste. The theme in the living room was Queen Anne–style furniture, and an original Monet hung on one wall. The Oriental rug covering the mahogany floors was so lush I wanted to kick off my shoes and walk barefoot on it, but I doubted my hostess would appreciate that.

Tamra sat down on a settee and patted the spot beside her. "I heard something about a fundraiser," she said. "What is the village up to now?"

She was so light and breezy with her conversation style I hardly noticed her condescending tone. I said the first thing that popped into my head. "They're updating their book collection in the school library at the elementary school. The old ones are dated and falling apart."

I had no idea whether it was true, but it sounded like a believable reason for my visit.

"That's just dreadful," she said in that same birdsong cadence. I could imagine her declaring the end of the world with the same airy tone. "I'm a huge fan of the written word."

"I hate to trouble you with it," I said.

"It's no bother at all. I'm rattling around this place with no one to talk to but James, and his interest in conversation is rather limited. To be honest with you, I'm happy for the diversion. So tell me, what's going on down in the village?"

It was the perfect opportunity, and one I wasn't about to waste. "Betty Wickline was murdered. Have you heard about that? You knew Betty, didn't you?"

She frowned, though no lines formed on her tightened features. "No, I can't say I recall the name."

"I believe she sat on the jury during your murder trial."

I'd been hoping for some kind of reaction, but all of the plastic surgery she'd had must have given Tamra an incredible poker face because her expression did not change in the slightest. "I don't dwell on the unpleasantness of the past," she said.

"Your attorney knew her," I said abruptly. "Someone spotted them talking right after the case."

"Then perhaps you should speak with him," she said softly, then added, "Ah, here's our coffee. You may pour, James."

It was an excellent brew, and there were the most delightful cookies on the tray as well. I found myself swept up in idle conversation, and only too late, I realized I'd told the woman much more about myself than she had told me about her. She was as skillful an interrogator as I'd ever seen. Sheriff Hodges could take lessons from her.

After our repast, she ushered me out the door without a single opportunity to follow up with more questions about Betty's death. The woman was smooth, I had to give her that.

As I was about to leave, James suddenly appeared with something in his hands. Tamra glanced at it, signed it, then gave it to me. "That should do nicely, don't you think?"

It was a check for five thousand dollars, made out to the Maple Ridge Library Book Fund. Blast it all, now I'd have to convince the principal that they needed new books, and somehow explain how I'd started this fundraiser in the first place without consulting her.

I wasn't ready to go home yet, though if we were going to eat on time, I'd have to get started making dinner pretty soon. Bill, bless his heart, had tried to learn to cook when he'd officially retired, but the only thing the man could make with any consistency were pancakes and scrambled eggs. He'd made a standing offer to me that any time I didn't want to cook or eat out, he'd provide the dinner, but it was a rare night I was willing to face either one of his specialties.

I wondered where I could find Betty's ex-husband, Larry Wickline. Butch had tracked him down at a bar, but I wasn't eager to brace the man in one myself. Not that I'm a teetotaler. I like the odd glass of wine on occasion, but I got mine from the grocery store, not from a pub. I scatted back to the shop to look up Larry's number in the phone book. Miracle of miracles, David was actually helping a customer at the cash register when I walked in! When she turned around, I saw that it was Cindy Maitland, one of the waitresses from the coffee shop.

"Don't mind me, I just need something in my office."

David was oblivious, but Cindy actually blushed. "I was just leaving."

"Don't rush off on my account." Gad, now I was driving customers away from my shop.

She said, "I was on my break, but I need to get back." As she was leaving, she turned to David and said, "I'll see you later."

"Okay. Come back any time."

After she was gone, I said offhandedly, "She's pretty, isn't she?"

"If you like redheads," he said absently.

"That's right, you prefer brunettes. Or should I say, one brunette in particular?"

"Don't start, Carolyn."

I wasn't going to let up, though. "David, sweet, dear David, I understand why you think Julia Roberts is beautiful. My lands, even *People* magazine thinks so. But she's married. With kids. You need to find someone more, well, for lack of a better word, attainable." David had one of the biggest crushes in the world on Julia Roberts. Hannah told me his room was wallpapered with posters from her movies and signed photographs he'd bought on eBay. Hannah had gotten so tired of watching her movies that she'd bought him a personal DVD player just so she wouldn't have to watch *Mystic Pizza* yet again.

"I just like her movies," he said stubbornly. "Now can we talk about something else? Anything else?"

"Fine, the lecture on your love life is officially over. How have our sales been?"

"Cindy was it. She bought one of your ornaments, so that's $2.95 in the till we didn't have before. What's wrong with these people, Carolyn? How could they imagine you had anything to do with Betty's murder?"

I patted his shoulder. "David, this will pass. We just need to ride it out. In the meantime, did you have any luck with that new signature color you've been looking for?"

"I don't know. I've got one kiln going right now. We'll see in the morning."

I glanced at the clock and saw that it was ten minutes until closing time. "Tell you what, why don't you go on home. I can close up tonight by myself."

"If it's all the same to you, I'd rather just stay here until my class tonight."

I took in his hangdog expression. "Things a little rough at home?"

"She's being so unreasonable. I never wanted to go to Travers in the first place. I'm a potter, Carolyn, not a student."

"Why can't you be both?" I asked. "You're getting a golden opportunity for a free education, and your mom's been pretty easygoing about you working here, too."

"Up until now. You've got to talk to her, explain to her that I'm doing something serious here."

"David, I'm afraid your mother and I have our own set of problems. I'm not going to do either of us any good if I start in about you."

The front door chimed, and I was honestly surprised to see Hannah walk in. "Were you two talking about me?"

David started to stammer out an answer when I cut him off. "Your ears must have been on fire. I'm guessing you're not here to throw a pot."

"Why, do you have an ugly one you want shattered? If you do, then I'm your gal."

"She meant on the pottery wheel, Mom."

Hannah turned to her son. "David, I know perfectly well what she meant."

"I've got some work to do in back," I said, "if you two will excuse me." It looked as though Hannah and David were going to have a heart-to-heart talk, and I didn't want to intrude.

"Stay, Carolyn. This involves you, too."

I shrugged and waited for what she had to say. Hannah nodded her approval, then looked at her son and said, "David, I've been talking to your professors at school."

"I can't believe you," David said loudly. "You can't do that, Mom."

"I can, and I did," she said. "They all say you're doing

wonderfully, by the way. I'm sorry I came down so hard on you last night."

The poor guy didn't know what hit him. Before he could say another word, Hannah looked me squarely in the eye and said, "I owe you an apology, too. I shouldn't have deserted you this morning, especially with what you're going through at the moment."

"There's nothing to apologize for," I said, then added with a grin, "but today was my turn to buy, so I'm afraid you're going to have to pick up the check tomorrow."

"Fair enough," she said.

David, clearly puzzled by what was going on, said, "I've got to go. I've got a class."

He tore out the door before we could get out our good-byes. Hannah waited a second, then started laughing. "That child can surely make an exit, can't he?"

"When he wants to. Are you sure we're okay?"

"Absolutely. He really is doing well in school. His advanced ceramics instructor told me David has a gift for glazes."

"I could have told you that myself. Listen, I don't have anything special planned for tonight, but would you like to have dinner with Bill and me? We'd love to have you."

"Thanks, but I've already got plans."

"A date, by any chance?" Hannah rarely went out, nearly always with disastrous results. She claimed she had bad luck when it came to men, and from what I'd seen, it was a fact I couldn't dispute. Even when I'd tried to fix her up, the evening had been a debacle.

"No, I really do have to wade through those Shake-speare essays. I've put them off as long as I dare. I'd love to take a rain check, though."

"Done."

After Hannah was gone, I ran the reports on our cash

register and transferred our meager funds from the till to
my "safe." Actually, I didn't have a real safe on the prem-
ises—I had a ceramic pig in the back room that I used for
one. No one in their right mind would suspect I was actually hiding my cash in a piggy bank.

I was almost ready to go home when I remembered
Larry Wickline. Some detective I was. I looked up his
number, called it, but got a busy signal. At least he was
home.

Just as I put the receiver back, the telephone rang in my
hand. "Hello?"

"That was fast," my husband said on the other end of
the line. "What were you doing, standing there waiting for
me to call?"

"What can I say, I'm psychic. You're calling about dinner, aren't you?" I swear, that man lived by his stomach.

"Yep, that's right. Sorry, but I'm running into some
problems with one of those dressers, so I'm going to work
here at Olive's shop. Don't worry about me tonight. I already ate."

"What did you have?"

"A salad."

I didn't have to see his face to know that he was lying.
"Okay, suddenly you're a worse liar than I am. Now what
did you really eat for dinner?"

He chuckled softly. "What's a salad have in it? Lettuce,
right? Well, I had lettuce."

Then I got it. "Did you have pickles and onions, too?
You ate a hamburger, didn't you?"

"I had the lettuce with it," he said stubbornly.

"Bill Emerson, you need to eat better than that, and you
know it. At least tell me you skipped the French fries."

He sounded almost smug as he said, "They went great
with the chocolate milkshake. Carolyn, I watch what I eat

most of the time, but sometimes I want a hamburger, some fries, and a shake, and I don't see any reason not to have them." He sounded so stubborn, I could almost see his pout.

"You know what? You're right. You're a grown man. Just don't make a habit of it."

There was a pause, then he said, "You gave in way too easy. What have you been up to?"

"I don't know what you're talking about."

"Hah. And you said I was a worse liar than you were. You've been snooping around town, haven't you?"

"I'm not going to dignify that remark with an answer."

His suddenly barked out a laugh. "That's because you can't."

"If you're finished braying, I have to figure out what I'm eating for dinner."

My husband's voice was contrite as he said, "I should have taken you out with me. You could have had a burger, too."

Usually I was pretty careful about watching what I ate, but with the stress I'd been under recently, a milkshake and burger might have been worth the calories. "Don't worry about me. I'll manage."

"You always do. If you need me, call me. And if you're at that shop of yours after dark, give me a buzz, and don't leave until I get there. You understand? Don't get all huffy, Carolyn. I'm just worried about you."

It was one of my husband's longer speeches, and I knew he meant well. "I'm locking up and heading out as soon as we get off the phone. I'll see you later."

"You can count on it," he said.

Since my husband had given in to one of his whims, I thought about what I'd like to eat if I were to ignore my worries about extra calories. A dessert dinner sounded great, filled with banana splits, hot fudge sundaes, and parfaits, but I knew I could never eat that kind of junk without feeling guilty about it. I decided to see what was in my refrigerator at home. As I grabbed my keys, I remembered Larry Wickline. Should I call him again, or leave it until morning? Chances were his line would still be busy, and then I could forget about him for the night with a clear conscience.

Blast it all, the man had the gall to pick up on the first ring. After his abrupt hello, I said, "Mr. Wickline, my name is Carolyn Emerson, and I just called to extend my sympathy on the loss of your wife." I figured if I made myself a sympathetic ear, he might be willing to talk about his ex.

"She was my ex-wife, and I've been celebrating since I heard the news."

I could hear the drunken tone in his voice. Maybe I could get him with his guard down, if I played it right. "If you don't mind my asking, why are you so happy about it?"

"Why? You're kidding, right? Are you sure you knew her? The woman was a hag, through and through."

I couldn't necessarily disagree with his assessment, but that hadn't been the role I'd chosen to play. "Surely there must have been something good about her. You married her, didn't you?"

"And I didn't live a single day after that I didn't regret it. But now she's gone."

"When was the last time you saw her?" I may have been pushing him a little too hard, but I was afraid he was going to get bored with me and hang up. One thing I knew. I was not going to that man's house while he was in a drunken state and brace him about his ex-wife. That would be a whole new level of foolishness, one I didn't want to reach.

"Gave her a check the day she died. She cashed it, can

you believe it? I guess I shouldn't mind. It was a going-away present, wasn't it?" Then he laughed so hard I thought he was going to drop the telephone. The laugh turned into a hacking cough, and I heard the phone hit the floor.

"Mr. Wickline? Are you all right?"

"Think I'm going to be sick," he said, and then he hung up on me. So Larry Wickline admitted seeing his ex-wife the day she died. That meant he had motive *and* opportunity, and anybody could have taken an awl from my shop and stabbed her as a means of murder.

But something was troubling me, something that had been nagging at the back of my mind all day. I still couldn't figure out why Betty had ended up in my shop in the first place. I was going about this all wrong. Instead of looking at who might want Betty dead, I should be trying to figure out why she was in my pottery shop when she had no right on earth to be there. If I knew that, it might just lead me to the murderer. Suddenly I wasn't in the mood to face the sparse offerings in my refrigerator.

It was time to visit Shelly.

"Well, look who slipped her leash. Out on the town by yourself?" Shelly Ensign smiled when I walked in the door of her café. She was a petite woman who ran her grill the way Patton disciplined his troops. The café had been decorated last in the fifties, with black and white tiles on the floor, red vinyl tabletops, and mismatched chairs throughout the place. It was just about the homiest place I'd ever eaten.

"Why don't you hand that spatula off to somebody else and join me?"

She smiled. "You're kidding, right? Nobody uses this

but me." Shelly touched the spatula lovingly for a second, then asked, "What would you like?"

I thought about getting a salad, honestly I did, but I found myself ordering a duplicate of my husband's dinner. Shelly laughed. "You two should have eaten together, since you're both having the same thing."

As I ate, Shelly took a second and came close to my seat at the bar. "How are you, Carolyn?"

"I've been better," I said. "How about you?"

She looked around. "Nobody's dumped any bodies here, so I'm doing better than you are. Anything I can do?"

"No, not unless you know who did it."

Shelly shook her head. "I have a suspect list that covers half of Maple Ridge, but I'm guessing you've got one like that yourself. Tell you what, I'll keep my ears open."

"I'd appreciate it."

I would have loved to chat more with her, but the dinner rush began and Shelly was soon lost in a blur of food prep.

I didn't have any insights by the time I left, but I did have a full belly.

At least that was something.

Chapter 5

"So what did you end up eating tonight?" Bill asked me as he walked in the house later that night.

"This and that. I didn't have a real meal," I said. Well, I didn't. I didn't consider a hamburger, fries, and a milkshake a real dinner. I wasn't about to admit that I'd matched his choices, though.

He misread the look of indigestion on my face for one of disapproval. "I let you down tonight, didn't I?"

"I'm a big girl," I said. And getting bigger by the meal. "I can fend for myself."

"Tell you what, tomorrow night, I'll take you out for a real meal. How does that sound?"

I was stuffed at the moment, and the thought of anything else to eat made me queasy. "We'll see."

Bill misread me again. Looking a little hurt, he said, "I said I'm sorry. Don't be that way."

"Fine. Dinner tomorrow night sounds fine." I didn't

mean to sound petulant, but what I needed was an antacid, not a dinner invitation.

"I'm not sure I want to go now," he said.

"Whatever," I said. I hurried to the bathroom medicine cabinet where we kept the Alka-Seltzer. I didn't want Bill to see me downing the stuff, especially after I'd scolded him for his eating habits.

As I finished drinking the antacid, I heard a tap on the door. "Carolyn, I'm sorry."

I rinsed the cup and put it back on the stand, then opened the door. "You don't have anything to apologize for."

"You forgive me, then?" He had a hurt look in his eyes that I couldn't stand.

I hugged him and said, "Always. Now let's change the subject, okay?"

"That's fine by me," he said, the hurt gone. "What did you do today?"

"Can we talk about something else?" I asked as I walked into the living room.

"Bad day at the shop?"

"You could say that," I said, not wanting to have this conversation either.

"But you weren't at the shop all day, were you?"

I bolted up off the couch. "Bill Emerson, have you been spying on me?"

"I popped in to say hi, but David told me you were gone. Nosing around, were you?"

"For your information, I was doing some charity work." I reached for my purse and plucked out Tamra's check. Waving it under his nose, I said, "If you must know, I've been raising money for new books for the elementary school library. You don't know as much as you think you do, buster."

He raised both palms toward me. "Sorry, I didn't mean anything by it. Hang on a second." He left the room for a minute, and when he came back, he had a fifty in his hands. "Here."

"What's that for?"

"More books. Don't worry, it's out of my chair money."

We lived off his retirement and my shop income, but Bill had allotted some of the money he made creating furniture as allowances for each of us. I'd resisted the idea at first, but it was nice for each of us to have some "mad" money to spend however we wanted.

"You don't need to do that," I said, suddenly feeling guilty about my deception.

"Don't have to. Want to." He said.

I had no choice but take the money, but I promised myself I'd match his donation. This investigation was costing me more than I thought.

The telephone rang just before bed, and I thought about ignoring it, but it could have been one of the boys, and I hated when I missed their calls.

"Carolyn, it's Kendra."

Great. Probably the last person in the world I wanted to talk to just before bed.

"It's pretty late, Kendra. Can't it wait until morning?"

"I thought you'd want to know what I found out," she said, managing to sound hurt.

"Sorry. I do appreciate you helping out."

"I won't keep you, but I've been asking around, on the sly of course, and I've come up with two possibilities."

After a long pause, I said, "I'm waiting."

"One is Malcolm Pickens at the bank."

"Malcolm? You're kidding me. I can't see him having an affair with anybody, let alone Betty." Malcolm was a bald, portly man with a gap-toothed smile, not that he ever brought it out much.

"That's not the half of it. You'll never believe who the other one is."

"Do I have to guess?" I asked. I swear, that woman could drive me crazy.

"It's none other than our dear sheriff, John Hodges."

"What? Are you sure?" I'd spoken to the sheriff twice since the murder, and he hadn't given the slightest indication that he'd been seeing Betty. Or had he? I had been in shock finding the body that night. I was so focused on myself that I hadn't really noticed what was going around me. And then I realized that Kendra might just have something. Hodges had lingered over Betty's body when he'd arrived, and he'd knelt beside her longer than it would take to check for a pulse. He'd even rubbed his eyes a little during our first talk, but he'd claimed it had been allergies, and I'd believed him. That put a whole new light on things. Maybe I wouldn't have to investigate after all. If Betty was his girlfriend, surely he'd want to find her killer. Then again, maybe he was convinced I'd done it. If that was the case, nothing would stop him from putting me away. It certainly cast a new set of shadows over the mess I was in.

"Carolyn, are you still there?"

"Sorry, I got lost in a thought for a second. Kendra, thanks for your help. I appreciate it."

"Any time," she said smugly.

Bill put his book aside and asked, "What was that all about?"

"Do you really want to know?"

He shook his head. "Nope, I really don't."

"Good, then I won't have to tell you."

When he saw I wasn't going to say anything, he finally said gruffly, "You can cross Malcolm off your list."

"I didn't think you wanted to talk about it."

"I don't." He sighed with obvious exasperation. "But I don't have much choice, do I?"

"Why couldn't Malcolm have done it?"

"He's been in Boston all week on vacation. I doubt he'd trot back up here just to knock Betty off."

I studied my husband a second, then asked, "And how did you happen to come across that information? You haven't been snooping, too, have you?"

"We both get our hair cut at People's Barbershop. He mentioned it last week when I went in for a trim." Bill reached over and turned off the light by his side of the bed. "Good night."

"Night," I said. So I could take Malcolm off my list. But that still left me Sheriff Hodges.

Whether it was because of my meal, some lingering memories of finding Betty's body in my shop, or the discovery that our sheriff may have been dating the murder victim, I had the oddest set of dreams and nightmares I'd ever had in my life that night. As a result, I didn't actually get much rest. I finally gave up trying to sleep at all a little after 4 A.M. I had another day of investigating ahead of me, and I was also going to have to go by the school and make my growing book-fund donation before the principal got wind of what I was up to.

Bill didn't even wake up as I dressed, and I thought about telling him I was going to Fire at Will early, but I knew he'd never get back to sleep if I did, and there was no sense in both of us being grumpy. Instead, I left him a note on my pillow, telling him where I'd gone.

I drove to the shop through the dark and quiet streets of town. It was almost surreal seeing the places I knew so well in the light of day, now dark and deserted.

I wasn't about to park in the upper lot so far away from

the store—not that early in the morning—but I couldn't bring myself to park right in front of the shop, either. Compromising, I tucked the Intrigue into an area a block away, in front of the now empty Emily's Donut World. The place had kept the same name under several different owners, but it never managed to stay open more than three months at a time. I was starting to think that businesses could be cursed, or at least locations.

Wrapping my coat around me, I walked briskly to Fire at Will. True to the weatherman's word, it was actually spitting snow, though from the look of it, there wouldn't be any accumulation. That was fine by me. I'd had more than my fill for the year and was ready for some warm weather.

In record time, I was safely behind locked doors again, but I resisted the urge to turn on the shop's lights. I didn't exactly want to advertise my presence to the world. Instead, I made my way to the back, and once the dividing door was shut between the paint-your-own area and the pottery wheels, I allowed myself a single light in my office. If I paid some bills and took care of a dozen other chores like reordering supplies and checking out the new catalogs, I might not feel quite so guilty deserting David later in the day to continue my investigation into Betty's murder.

Wanting to spend my time wisely, I struggled to balance the company checkbook, but it was no use. I was too tired. Why hadn't I been able to sleep at home? I knew that if I didn't get some rest, I was going to be crabby the entire day. So I grabbed a comforter from the closet and stretched out on the couch near my office. Just as I settled down to sleep, I heard what sounded like an explosion in front of the shop.

· · ·

Without thinking, I threw the dividing door open and raced toward the front of the store. In hindsight, I realized I should have used the back exit and called the police from my cell phone, but I wasn't exactly thinking clearly. Flipping on the light, I saw a figure through the broken front window retreating into the darkness. What had he been trying to do, get in my shop in search of something? Or was he just trying to scare me off? If it was the latter, he was doing a darn fine job of it. The front window display was a ruined mess, and shards of glass lay everywhere. A tumbled old brick lay in the middle of the debris. Whoever had done this hadn't been a big fan of subtlety. I reached for a broom, my natural reaction to any untidiness, then decided I'd better call the police before I touched anything.

I had to give Sheriff Hodges's staff some credit; someone arrived minutes after I hung up. Instead of the sheriff, though, a young patrolwoman pulled up in front of the shop.

I saw that her name badge said "Sally Jones" as I watched her take in the shattered window. She turned to me and asked, "Are you all right?"

"To be honest with you, I'm angry more than anything else. Can I clean this mess up now?"

"Let me get a few pictures first. Do you mind turning on more lights?"

"No, that's no problem at all."

After she'd taken photos of the scene, she said, "You can clean it up, but you might want to wait until your insurance agent gets here. He'll want to see it for himself."

At least the snow had stopped, though the predawn wind was icy. "I never thought about that. I suppose I'll have to file a claim, won't I?"

"It's up to you. You might want to see how much it would be to replace the window yourself before you call anybody, though. That way your premiums won't go through the roof. I need to ask you a few questions. Were you here when this happened?"

I nodded. "I was in back. I decided to come in early and pay some bills. You know, get an early jump on things. Nobody knew I was here."

"At least not that you're aware of." She looked at me for a second before she jotted my response down in her notebook. "Is there any reason you can think of why someone would do this?"

"No, nothing I can put my finger on."

She nodded. "It's probably just a random act of vandalism. We get them occasionally, even in Maple Ridge." The officer almost looked guilty as she added, "I've got to call the sheriff. Since the murder happened here earlier, we've got a red flag on your business. I'm sorry, but I don't have any choice."

"I understand. You're just doing your job."

She nodded her thanks, then spoke into her radio. "Audrey, you need to wake the sheriff up."

"I already did when the call came in," the dispatcher replied. "He's on his way."

Less than a minute later I saw flashing lights approaching. At least he hadn't used his siren.

Hodges took in the shattered glass and the broken pottery, then nudged the brick that had been used with his foot. "Must have made a whale of a noise."

"I thought the roof was caving in," I admitted.

"You were here when it happened?" He looked surprised.

"I was catching up on some paperwork," I replied. Now the whole world would know I had insomnia.

"You were lucky," he said.

I looked at the mess in the floor. "Oh yes, I feel like I just won the lottery."

"You're alive, aren't you?" He looked over at Sally and said, "You can go back on patrol. I've got it from here. Did you get some shots of this?"

"Yes, sir. I'd be glad to finish up and write the report."

"I said I've got it. Get back on the streets, officer."

"Yes, sir." She nodded to me, then left.

It might not have been the best time to say something about Betty Wickline, but I figured I might not get another chance when there was no one else around. "I'm really sorry about Betty."

"I bet you are," he said. Then he looked at me, and he must have seen something in my eyes. "What?"

"I've heard you two were close. Very close." Okay, it wasn't subtle, but then again, neither was a brick through my plate-glass window.

"I don't know what you think you know, but you'd better drop it, and I mean right now."

I tried to keep my voice soft as I said, "By the way, how's your wife?"

"Evelyn's fine," he snapped. "Carolyn Emerson, if I hear one more word of this nonsense from you or anybody else, I'll lock you up, do you understand me?"

"On what grounds, littering? I'll clean this mess up as soon as you're gone. I can't help what folks in town are saying about you and Betty Wickline."

Hodges ran a hand through his hair. "Oh man, Evelyn is not going to be happy about this. She and Betty never got along."

I nodded in sympathy. "It's got to be especially hard on her. Does she know about you two?"

"Blast it, there's nothing to know! I wasn't having an affair with Betty Wickline. You've got to be out of your mind for even suggesting it."

"I never said a word about it myself. I heard it through the grapevine."

"You should know better than to listen to idle gossip. Do you honestly think I could stand the thought of being around that woman for more than ten minutes at a time? You've all lost your minds if you believe that."

He started back to his patrol car when I asked, "So, what are you going to do about this?"

He shook his head. "It was a prank gone bad, Carolyn. Don't be so paranoid."

"Then why did they hit my shop and not Rose Colored Glasses or Hattie's Attic?"

"Like I said, you were just lucky, I guess," he answered, then got into his car and drove away.

Yeah, right. Then why didn't I feel all that lucky? I hated to do it, but I had to call Bill. He'd want to know, and besides, I could get his advice on what to do about the insurance claim. My business did pretty well—at least it had before the murder—but I couldn't afford an increase in my premiums.

He answered on the ninth ring. I said, "Honey, it's me."

"Where are you? I thought you were still in bed with me." Bill's voice was groggy, and in my mind I could see him sitting up in bed rubbing his eyes.

"I couldn't sleep, so I came down to the shop to pay some bills. Bill, I need you to focus. Are you awake?"

"Of course I am. I'm talking to you, aren't I?" Then a chill hit his voice. "Carolyn, are you all right?"

"I'm fine, but somebody threw a brick through the front window of my shop."

"Were you hurt?" No doubt about it, he was awake now, the poor dear.

"I'm fine, but I've got a mess on my hands. Can you come down here?"

"I'll be there in three minutes. Call the police."

"I already did. They've come and gone."

"What did they say?"

"Hodges thinks it was a random act of vandalism."

"That blamed fool wouldn't know a crime if it happened in his living room."

"I'd be happy to discuss this with you when you get here, but can it wait till then? I'm freezing."

"Of course it can." He hung up without saying good-bye, but I didn't care. I just wanted him beside me so I could deal with this violation of my business without worrying that someone was still out there in the shadows, watching the entire thing unfold.

"Thank God you're all right," my husband said as he hugged me close. I'd held myself rigid until he'd arrived, but the moment he wrapped his arms around me, I melted.

I was just about to say something sweet to him when he added, "What in the world were you thinking, coming down here by yourself in the middle of the night? Have you lost your mind?"

Suddenly his embrace wasn't all that warm. I pulled away from him. "It's nearly 6 A.M.. On what planet is that the middle of the night? I had work to do here, and since I couldn't sleep, I decided to get an early start."

"Why didn't you at least wake me up? I'd have come down here with you."

"Because I don't need a chaperone, an escort, or a bodyguard," I snapped. "I left you a note."

I could see in his eyes that he knew he'd pushed me too far. "Okay, take it easy. I'm just glad you weren't hurt."

"I was in the back room, Bill. That brick couldn't have hit me unless it had been shot out of a cannon."

"I'm not talking about the brick. I'm talking about the lunatic who threw it. What if he had more on his mind than shattering your storefront window?"

I didn't want to think about that, and I was saved from answering when a familiar car drove up. It was Butch Hardcastle in a brand new Cadillac, and I wondered yet again if the driver had fully given up his life of crime. Butch nodded to Bill as he entered the shop, then looked at me intently. "I don't see any cuts or scrapes. You okay?"

"I'm fine," I said. "How did *you* hear about what happened?"

"I've got a police scanner by my bed," he said. "It helps me sleep at night."

"Is that the only reason you have it on?" I asked.

"Why else?" He dismissed me and turned to my husband. "Were you with her when this happened?"

"No, she didn't wake me up when she left the house."

I could see Butch's expression darken, but I wasn't about to listen to another lecture. "Before you say a word, I'm a grown woman, and I won't change my life because of what happened to Betty Wickline. This window would have been shattered whether I'd been here or not. Who knows, I may have stopped a robbery when I turned on the light."

Butch shook his head. "No offense, Carolyn, but what is there here that's worth stealing? Don't get me wrong, I love this place, but it wouldn't be at the top of my list of establishments to rob. If I was still in the business, I mean."

"Where would you hit first?" Bill asked.

"That's an interesting question. I've thought about it some—just idle speculation, if you know what I mean—but I think I'd hit Balmark's."

"The sporting-goods store? I thought the jewelry store or the bank would be your first choice."

Butch said, "No, they have pretty sophisticated alarms, and some heavy-duty security systems. Too tough to crack as a one-man job. I'd go to Balmark's and wait in the bathroom just before they closed. There's a drop ceiling in there, and after the employees were gone, I'd fill up a few bags of their pricier stuff, hit their joke of a safe in back, and still be home before midnight."

"Wow, I would never have thought of that."

He shrugged, and managed to hide most of his pride. "It takes a professional to look at these things with a seasoned eye."

"If you two are finished with your larcenous daydreams, I need help cleaning this mess up."

"We were just talking," Bill said. "I thought you were going to call Bob?" Bob Davis was our insurance agent, a man who was still mostly a boy. Bob had taken over the business from his father, and I wasn't at all sure being an insurance agent was what Bob wanted to be when he grew up.

"You don't want to call him," Butch said. "I know a guy who owes me a favor. We can have this glass replaced before you open, and he'll do it for half the price anybody else in the county would charge."

"I don't want you to use your connections on my account," I said. Even to my ears, my words sounded a little stuffy.

"No, this is legit. I helped the guy out with a problem he had, and now it's his turn to do me a favor."

"What did you do, beat somebody up for him?" Bill asked.

Butch laughed. "You've been watching too much late-night TV. One of his employees was stealing from him, so he asked for my help. I had the guy pegged in twenty minutes. He was a real amateur. Just let me make a call."

Butch stepped away from us as he pulled out his cell phone. "I'm not sure about this," I told Bill.

"The man wants to help. You should let him."

I punched my husband's shoulder lightly. "And you. What was with all that burglary talk? Are you thinking about taking up a new hobby?"

"I don't get out much," he said. "You've got this shop where you meet lots of people, but since I retired, I spend most of my time in my workshop by myself."

"You could always come work for me."

He put one hand behind his ear and said, "Listen, do you hear that?"

"What?" I couldn't hear a thing.

"Unless you hear oinks coming from the sky and pigs are up there doing barrel rolls, don't look for me to sign on."

"David says I'm a good boss," I said, a little hurt by his comment.

"You're a better wife," he said. "I don't think we could stand being around each other twenty-four hours a day."

I laughed. "You're probably right. Let's get this mess cleaned up before Butch's friend gets here."

I reached for the brick, but my hand hesitated of its own accord. Was I honestly afraid to touch it? Bill must have been watching me. "Let me get that."

"No, it's fine," I said as I retrieved it. Instead of throwing it into the trash can—which had been my intent—I carried it back and put it on my desk. If I needed a spur to find out who had murdered Betty Wickline, the brick would serve as a constant reminder.

Bill had donned a pair of my thick, insulated gloves and

was putting the biggest shards of glass into an empty box. "I've just about got the big stuff taken care of."

I joined him and picked out the pottery pieces that hadn't been ruined by the brick or the shattering glass. My ornaments were nearly unbreakable, but I was afraid I couldn't say that about the rest of the pieces I'd had on display. Two of the dishes Robert Owens had made were broken beyond repair, and David's face jug was shattered. Oddly enough, Martha's vase was fine. I collected the shards of the broken pieces and set them aside. They'd live again in mosaics, but I hated to see the destruction. All at once, I was angry again at whoever had done this.

"Trouble?" Butch asked as he walked back to me.

"No, I just hate to see such waste."

"Yeah, it's a real shame." His expression brightened. "I've got good news. Jim Hickman will be out here in ten minutes to get some measurements, and the new window's as good as in. Can I buy you two some breakfast in the meantime?"

"No, I have to stay with the store. Thank you, Butch. I really appreciate your help."

"Hey, it's the least I can do. Well, if you're sure you two don't need me, I've got something I need to take care of."

Bill looked at his watch. "This early in the morning?"

Butch put a finger to his lips, and Bill nodded. After he was gone, I asked my husband, "What was that about?"

"I don't know, but to be honest with you, I was kind of afraid to ask."

"Butch has a kind heart."

Bill nodded. "He seems like a good guy, but I wouldn't want him mad at me."

I grinned. "Then be good to me."

"I don't need to be threatened to do that."

"I know you don't."

Butch was as good as his word, and when I saw his friend's quote for a new window, I wished I'd hugged him before he left.

After Mr. Hickman had gone to get the glass and a helper to install it, Bill said, "I'm hungry."

"Then go eat." My stomach had been rumbling, too, but there was no way I could leave my place unguarded. I wrapped my coat tighter around me and turned the heat up yet again. My small gas furnace couldn't touch the chilly temperature in the shop, but at least it might keep some of my supplies from freezing solid until the window was installed.

"I'm not leaving here without you." The stubbornness was thick in his voice, and I knew it was pointless to argue with him.

Five minutes later, a van pulled up, and I felt Bill tense beside me. What was this about? To my surprise, a harried young man popped out of the driver's side and handed us two bags and a tray holding two cups.

"What's this?" I asked as I accepted the offering.

"Breakfast from O'Daniel's," he said.

"But we didn't order anything."

"That's okay, it's taken care of." He glanced at the bill, then added, "A Mr. Hardcastle arranged it."

Under that gruff exterior, Butch really was a softy.

Bill and I took the food inside and ate at one of the work tables. In an odd sort of way it was fun, kind of like an arctic picnic. As we finished eating, I said, "We should do this more often."

"What, get vandalized, then sit around in the freezing cold waiting for repairs?"

I threw a wadded-up napkin at him. "Don't be silly. I mean have picnics like we used to do when we were dating."

He grinned at me. "I never told you this, but the reason we had so many picnics was because I couldn't afford to take you out anywhere. I figured if I raided my folks' pantry, it would be a cheap date."

"And here I thought I married a romantic."

"You did," he said. "Just not a rich one."

"I feel rich enough, thank you very much."

The window was installed twenty minutes before it was time to open, and Bill hadn't left my side, though his fidgeting was starting to drive me crazy.

"Don't take this the wrong way," I told him, "but don't you have somewhere else to be? Anywhere else?"

"You tired of me already?"

I patted his arm. "I appreciate you staying with me, but I'm fine. Honestly."

He nodded. "Okay, I can take a hint. I'll go."

I hugged him again, then kissed him soundly. "Thank you. For everything. I don't know what I'd do without you."

"Don't worry, as long as I have any say about it, you won't have to."

Chapter 6

"I can't believe I missed all of the excitement," David said when he came in ten minutes after Bill left. "Why didn't you call me, Carolyn?"

"I had enough people here as it was," I said. "There wasn't anything you could do to help."

"Did you at least take a picture?"

"I suppose you could ask the police for one, if you really want to see the carnage. They took dozens of photographs." There must have been something cutting in my voice, because he looked at me as if he'd just been slapped.

"I'm sorry, Carolyn, I was just curious."

Wonderful; just because I was aggravated over the attack, I had no excuse for taking it out on David. "I know you were. Forgive me if I'm a little on edge."

"You should be happy about this," he said.

Was the boy on some kind of medication? "Which part should make me glad, the bill I just got for the replacement window, or the pottery pieces that were destroyed?"

"I'm talking about the reason the window was broken in the first place. You must have hit a nerve with somebody yesterday for them to try to scare you off so dramatically."

"And wouldn't it be nice if I knew which one I tweaked?" He was right, but without any idea of who had done it, I was back where I'd started.

Herman Meadows walked in and scowled at the window as he approached me. "I'm not paying for this," he said. "It's your responsibility as the tenant."

"I've already got it covered," I said as sweetly as I could. I'd wondered when my landlord would show up, and he hadn't disappointed me with his promptness.

"Carolyn, are you going to take this as a warning and stop nosing around in this murder thing?"

I was so happy to have somebody agree with me besides David, I leaned forward and kissed his cheek. "Thank you. I've been telling everyone this was a warning, but no one would believe me."

"I believe you," my assistant said sullenly.

Herman wiped his cheek with a blue bandana. "Have you completely lost your mind? I tell you that some maniac is trying to scare you off, and you kiss me!"

"I'll be careful," I said. "I promise."

"But will you stop?"

"Not on your life. I'm going to find out who killed Betty Wickline."

"Or die trying," he added.

"I certainly hope not, but I do appreciate your concern. Thanks for stopping by."

He looked at the window again, then said, "They did a good job, and fast, too. Who did you use?"

"Jim Hickman."

He shook his head. "He's good all right, but it's going to cost you a fortune."

I was tempted to tell him about the deal Butch had gotten me, but then I decided to keep that to myself, since Jim had done it as a favor. "I'm willing to pay it to have a window."

He nodded his approval. "That's why I love having you as a tenant. You understand the way things work."

After he left, I was rearranging the front window display when I heard a hard tap on the glass. As I looked up, I hoped that Jim Hickman had secured the window safely in place.

It was Robert Owens, the errant potter from North Carolina, and from the scowl on his face, I could tell that something other than my display skills was troubling him. Robert's unruly brown hair was as ruffled as ever. He was a tall, thin man with a potter's thin, wiry fingers, and with that artistic brooding he sported, I doubted many of the coeds at Travers could resist him.

When he walked in, he snapped, "What happened, Carolyn? That was supposed to be a set. I told you that I don't sell my pieces individually."

"That's fine with me," I said. "I'll pull the rest of your pieces from the display." I couldn't believe the tone of voice he was taking with me after the morning I'd had. "Do you want the shards from the broken pieces, too?"

"Shards?" he screamed. "You broke some of my pottery?"

"I didn't; the brick coming through the plate-glass window this morning did."

That certainly got his attention. "Why would somebody throw a brick through your window? Do you think they were targeting my pottery?"

This guy's ego was unbelievable. "I'm sure that's it. It probably doesn't have anything at all to do with the murder the other night."

He looked as though his eyes were going to pop right out of his skull. "Murder? Who was murdered?"

"Betty Wickline," I said. "You got to know her pretty well in the few weeks you've been in town, didn't you?" Okay, it was a total stab in the dark, and a mean thing to say at that, but I didn't appreciate him jumping down my throat.

For a split second, I thought he was going to cry. Then he reined in his expression before I could even be sure I'd seen it. "I knew her but not all that well. Who do the police suspect?"

"I'm pretty high on their list," I admitted, "but then again, so is anybody who has a key to the place, including you."

"I was in North Carolina," he said hastily. "Surely the police can't suspect me."

"Robert, you don't know our sheriff. If I were you, I'd line up an alibi, and I'd do it pretty darn fast."

He scowled. "I don't owe you an explanation or an alibi, either."

"Hey, I'm not the one asking. I just thought I'd give you a heads-up. You do still have the key I gave you, don't you?"

He looked down at his hands. "Actually, I lost it just before I left town. It was on my key ring, I would swear to that, but when I checked before going back to Carolina, I noticed that it was gone."

How convenient for him. "And you didn't think to call me so I could change the lock?"

"There was no time," he said. "I had to leave in a hurry."

I don't know what he was expecting, but I doubt it was the broad smile I gave him.

He asked, "Why the smile?"

"I can't wait to hear you tell Sheriff Hodges that you

lost your key. Do me a favor, call him now, would you? I'm willing to bet he'll trot right over here to meet you."

Robert shook his head. "If he wants to talk to me, he can track me down himself. I didn't have anything to do with the murder."

"I hope for your sake that's true." He started for the door, and I called out, "Hey, where are you going?"

"I've got a class to teach at Travers. Could I have another key, please?"

I had to hand it to him, the man had nerve. "I could give you one, but it wouldn't do you any good. I'm having the locks changed today." I'd wanted it done yesterday, but Clara Harper had been on vacation, and she was the only locksmith I trusted with my place.

"Fine, but I expect to have another key if I'm going to be teaching here."

"I'm sure you do," I said. I wasn't at all sure I wanted Robert Owens on my staff anymore, but I didn't need to decide his fate at that moment.

After he'd gone, I pulled the rest of his pieces from the display per his request, though it was really out of spite more than anything else. I didn't know who he thought he was, but I wasn't about to let him use that tone of voice with me, certainly not in my own shop. I sighed wistfully as I moved the last intact dishes to a back rack. Why couldn't David come up with a glaze that danced like Robert Owens's work did? I didn't doubt in time he'd do just that, but for now, my display case had a hole that needed to be filled. I searched through the inventory in our little gallery for something worthy of the window, but nothing grabbed my eye. I couldn't leave it like that, though. Then I had an idea. Why replace it at all? I took some white cardboard from the back, scrawled out a note in my most stylish handwriting style, then propped the sign up in place of Robert's dishes.

David was standing outside as I put it in place, and he was smiling as he came in. "That's a cool idea. I love it."

"Thanks." In black Sharpie, I'd written, "Imagine Your Work Here" on the placard. I walked outside to study it and was quite happy with the results. It might even bring some customers back into my shop, something I hadn't been able to accomplish with much success since the murder.

"So what's the verdict? Are you going to keep digging into Betty Wickline's murder?"

"No, for a change of pace, let's try to get some folks in here and paint some pottery."

"Sounds good to me," he said.

Now, if I could just figure out how to do that. It was too soon to offer the local schools another deal. It would be hard to get most adults here in the middle of the day, but there was a group I hadn't tapped yet, one I'd been aching to try to get into my place. I picked up the phone and dialed.

"Maple Ridge Center," a cultured woman's voice said after only one ring.

"Maggie Hicks," I replied. Maggie was the director at the senior center, and a friend since she'd first moved to town when we'd been in the second grade.

"One moment, please," the woman said, and I was put on hold, listening to Muzak that put my teeth on edge. Thankfully Maggie didn't keep me waiting long.

"Hello, Maggie Hicks."

Disguising my voice, I said, "Dearie, would you put me back on hold? They were playing the most delightful tune."

Maggie paused, then said, "Certainly."

Before I could tell her I was joking, she put me on hold

again. I couldn't take another second of the watered-down pap, so I hung up and hit the redial button on my phone.

After the elegant voice identified the center again, I lied. "I got cut off. Could you give me Maggie's office again?"

"Certainly," she said. Now how on earth had she managed to sound skeptical of my explanation with just one word?

"Maggie Hicks."

"Don't hang up, and for God's sake, whatever you do, don't put me on hold again."

My friend whooped with delight. "That was you? How funny. The music's dreadful, isn't it? I've been trying to get the owners to change it to something more contemporary, but they actually claim to like it. Can you imagine?"

That was Maggie, or Mile-a-Minute Maggie, as we'd called her in school. "Honestly? No. Listen, I need a favor."

"Spill. I heard about your front window at the shop. What's the world coming to?"

I didn't need to ask her how she'd heard. Maple Ridge had a backdoor communications community that would put the CIA to shame. I'd been counting on the gossip hotline to give me more than it had about Betty Wickline. The woman must have been an operative herself; she was that good at hiding her tracks.

"I couldn't honestly say, but at least I got a new window, so I don't have to knock the icicles off the pottery anymore. How squeamish would some of your folks be to come down here to the scene of a murder? I'll give them half off my regular group rates just to fill the place up again. If you'd rather not bring it up, that's fine with me, too. I understand completely."

"Come on, Carolyn, I'd be delighted to ask around.

Could it be today? We were supposed to have a sing-along
with Penny Pladgett, but the poor thing broke a hip and
she's back in the hospital."

"Today sounds great," I said. "And you don't think
they'll mind about the murder?"

"Are you kidding me? Some of them will probably
come because of it. How soon should we be there, and how
many can you take?"

We could handle twenty-four adults, but I wanted to
keep it below our maximum. "How about twenty? You can
make it any time, just give me half an hour's notice."

"You've got it. I'll call you back in a minute."

David had been eavesdropping on the tail end of my
phone call, and as I hung up, he was smiling. "That's one
way to get a full house."

"I know you don't approve of discounts, but I need to
see some faces here, you know? It's been entirely too long
since we've heard the sound of laughter."

"Hey, I'm all for it," he said. "I couldn't agree with you
more. What shall we pull out, the saucer collection?" We
normally reserved the mass-produced saucers for our
group discounts.

"What the heck, let's splurge and bring out the mugs."
We bought them wholesale from a supplier in New Hamp-
shire, but even with our deep discount, we'd still have trouble breaking even on what I was charging Maggie.

"Let's not go overboard," David said. I swear, sometimes he watched the bottom line closer than I did.

"What do you suggest?"

"We've got that order of salad plates we haven't used.
Why not pull them out?"

"Fine, that's probably a better idea. Let's set things up,
shall we?"

We'd just laid out the glazes and brushes at each station

when the telephone rang. "Carolyn? Hey, it's Maggie. I've got twenty-two. Is that okay? I didn't have the heart to tell anyone they couldn't come."

"That's fine. When are you coming?"

"As soon as we can load the bus, if you don't mind."

"Bring them on," I said.

It would be great having some activity in Fire at Will again, something that had nothing to do with Betty Wickline's murder.

The place was a wreck after the seniors left, but David and I were both smiling. They'd been full of energy and had a thousand questions for us. Most of the women had responded to David with broad smiles, something that had obviously embarrassed him a little. I felt a bit like a girl myself as four of the men took turns flirting with me.

"That was fun," I said as David and I wiped the tables.

"Where do they get the energy? I'm worn out."

"They're full of life, aren't they?"

David nodded. "If it's okay with you, after we clean up, I'm going to lunch."

"Are you that hungry?" I glanced at the clock and saw that David was an hour early for his break.

"No, I'm going to go out to my car and take a nap! If I don't show up in an hour, come wake me up."

My stomach rumbled a little after David left, and I wished I'd asked him to hang around until I could grab something and bring it back to eat. I thought about calling somebody from the Firing Squad to pick up something for me, but I didn't want to talk about the murder, and I was sure whoever I called would want to discuss it. I still had a rosy glow from the seniors' visit, and I didn't want to tarnish it with a discussion about the homicide.

I'd just about come to terms with my growling stomach when I saw a friendly face peering in through the front window, with a take-out bag from Shelly's Café in her hand.

"Have you eaten yet? I took a chance and ordered for two."

I didn't know which I was happier to see: that bag of food or my best friend Hannah's smiling face.

"We really are okay, aren't wc?" I asked Hannah as I finished off my club sandwich. She knew how to make things right between us. I was a sucker for a club, as long as there wasn't any tomato on it. Okay, I know, I'm not a purist, but that's how I've always liked mine.

"It's the best way I know to say I'm sorry. I shouldn't have taken my frustrations with David out on you."

I took a sip from one of the Cokes I'd provided from my small fridge in back. "Maybe it would be better if we didn't talk about him."

Hannah frowned. "No, I don't see how we'd be able to do that. He's too big a part of both our lives to just ignore. Think what an awkward gap his absence would leave in our conversations."

"More like a canyon," I agreed. "So, what would you like to talk about? I'm open to just about any topic except Betty Wickline."

Hannah bit her lip, then said, "That leaves another pretty large hole for us, doesn't it?"

She had a point. "I was hoping to avoid it, but you're right. Do you think the shattered window was tied into my snooping, too?"

Hannah nearly choked on her soft drink. "What happened? Did someone vandalize your home?"

"It happened here at the shop this morning," I explained. "Do you mean to tell me that David didn't call and tell you?"

"Fire at Will is kind of a sore subject between us at the moment," she admitted. "He should have called me anyway, though. Which window did they break?"

"The most expensive one, of course. Luckily, one of my Firing Squad members has a friend in the glass business, so he was able to get right to it."

Hannah shook her head. "I don't even have to guess which one, do I? It's the crook."

"Reformed crook," I said. After all Butch had done for me, including the window and the breakfast that morning, I wasn't going to let someone trash him, not even Hannah.

"Sorry, I know he's your friend. If it matters, David likes him, too."

I took Hannah's hand in mine. "With character references like that, you should at least keep an open mind about him. His best friend is Judge Blake. If she's not good enough for you, I don't know what I can say to change your mind."

"Let's just say I'll try not to judge him based on what I've heard, or what he used to do for a living. How's that?"

"I can live with that, and I'm sure Butch would accept those terms, too." The conversation had gotten much more serious than I liked, especially after we'd so recently patched up our friendship.

Hannah finished her sandwich, then said, "Carolyn, if you'd like to talk about your suspect list, I'd be glad to listen. It might help you figure out who you've irritated enough to move to violence."

"I couldn't even start to list the people I've annoyed. I'm not sure I have enough paper."

She smiled. "I mean lately."

"So do I."

"It couldn't hurt."

She wasn't going to give up, I could see that. Well, it just might help to tell her what I'd been up to. After all, Hannah had a more orderly mind than I did, and maybe she'd be able to offer me an objective opinion. "Okay, let's see. So far, my suspect list includes Robert Owens, Tamra Gentry, Larry Wickline, and Sheriff Hodges."

She looked at me intently to see if I was kidding, and when she saw that I was deadly serious, she asked, "Is there any reason you think the sheriff really might have killed her?"

"The two of them may have been having an affair."

Hannah whistled softly. "If that's true, then you've got to include Evelyn in your list, too."

"I hadn't even thought about that, but you're right." I was trying to narrow my list of suspects, not broaden it.

Hannah frowned. "I can see why Larry Wickline made your list, but why Tamra Gentry and Robert Owens?"

"Betty might have been blackmailing Tamra, and as for Robert, he had a key to the shop. That alone makes him a suspect. When I pressed him on knowing Betty, he got a little flustered. I keep thinking there had to be some reason why she was here in the first place. She could have been meeting Robert for a tryst, and something went wrong."

"It's possible," Hannah said. "But I thought his tastes ran to coeds, not their mothers."

"Maybe he's an equal-opportunity letch. It's worth looking into."

Hannah walked to the window that had just been replaced and looked out. "Is there anybody else?"

I wasn't sure whether she was joking, but I started thinking about other possibilities. "I guess you could include just about anybody here on the brook walk."

"That certainly pads your list, doesn't it?"

Something suddenly struck me. "Oh, blast it all."

"What's wrong? What did I say?"

"I just remembered. There are more keys floating around out there than I told the sheriff. Kendra Williams and I swapped keys last year when Bill and I went to North Carolina on a pottery tour of Seagrove. She came over and checked on the place when you and David were in England."

"Surely you don't think Kendra would kill Betty."

I threw my hands up in the air. "That's the problem. I don't know who's capable of murder."

"Given the right circumstances, I honestly believe that just about anybody is."

Her answer shocked me. "Even you?"

"To protect my son, I might. How about you?"

I thought about either one of my sons in jeopardy, and realized that she was probably right. "It's hopeless, isn't it? If Hodges can't figure it out, what chance do I have?"

"Don't forget, the sheriff doesn't have your resources. And if it's true that he was having an affair with Betty, he might not be the most objective investigator. I don't see how you have much choice, Carolyn. I was against it at first, but I see now that you need to keep digging."

She was right, but I was sick of trying to figure out who wanted Betty Wickline dead. It was time for a little diversion. "Enough of this murder talk. If you've got some time, David just finished firing some new bowls for our paint-your-own section. Would you like do one yourself?"

She laughed at that. "You know the artistic gene skipped me. My mother's a fabulous watercolorist, and David's got a real knack for ceramics, but I can't draw a stick figure."

"So create some modern art. You don't have to have a theme to paint a bowl. It's fun."

She glanced at her watch, then said, "I'm tempted, but I've got to get back to Travers. I'm glad we did this."

"Me, too," I said. I hugged her. "Thanks for coming by with lunch."

"Thanks for not throwing me out."

"Are you kidding me?" I asked. "I'd never do that to my best friend in the world. Besides, you had food."

"Ah, the magic ticket," she said with a smile.

"It can be."

Ten minutes after Hannah left, David stormed into the shop. I frowned at him. "What's wrong with you?"

"I saw her in here. Don't try to deny it. She's been spying on me again, hasn't she?"

"Are you talking about your mother?"

"Of course I am! What did she want? Did she grill you on where I was?"

I put my hands on his shoulders. "David, your mother was here to see me, as hard as that might be for you to believe. She came by with lunch to say she was sorry."

"Why doesn't she apologize to me, too? I deserve one as much as you do." He looked at me a few seconds, then said, "Aren't you going to respond?"

"To that? I don't think so. I've decided the only way I'm going to stay in both your good graces is to keep out of your lives. So that's what I'm going to do."

His frown started to crack into a smile as I added, "Well, I am. It's true. At least I'm going to try."

He was in a much better mood all afternoon. Maybe the little tantrum had done him some good.

That's what I was hoping, at any rate.

• • •

I wasn't happy with the front window arrangement, and since we weren't exactly overwhelmed with customers, I decided to make it my afternoon project. I added some pieces and removed others, but it still wasn't quite right. The only thing I was really pleased with was the sign I'd placed there on impulse. More times than not, when I went with my gut, I was happiest. However, I tended to over-analyze things sometimes, and those instances almost always led to disaster.

I was standing outside for the zillionth time trying to come up with something that would make the display grab potential customers when I nearly knocked down a woman who was passing behind me.

"Evelyn, I didn't see you there," I told the sheriff's wife as I took a step back. "I'm so sorry."

"I'm fine," she said. Evelyn Hodges was a solid woman, both in stature and disposition. There was nothing flashy about her, but she was a good person at heart. At least the woman I knew was. What would possess the sheriff to have an affair with Betty Wickline, unless he was looking for a little flash in his life?

"Nonsense. I nearly ran you down. Won't you come into the shop? I have coffee brewing."

She looked at Fire at Will as though it were a leper hospital. "No, I couldn't."

Evelyn tried to sidestep me, but I moved with her. "I'm sorry, I wasn't thinking. Were you and Betty close?"

"Close?" she hissed at me. "We were never friends." Her eyes narrowed as she added, "She brought it on herself. I won't shed any crocodile tears for her."

I stood there in shock as Evelyn hurried away. Had she really just said that? I wished I'd had a witness, a tape recorder, a stenographer, anything to record her words. I'd discounted the idea that the sheriff had been having an affair, but Evelyn's words had brought it right back to the front again. She clearly hated Betty Wickline—although that didn't mean she'd killed her.

On the other hand, it didn't mean she hadn't.

It was time to do a little more digging into the situation.

I was still standing on the curb, trying to collect my thoughts, when David came out.

"You've got a call." He must have spotted my expression of disbelief over what I'd just heard, because he added, "Are you all right?"

"What? I'm fine. Who's on the telephone?"

"It's Martha Knotts. She says she needs to talk to you. It's important."

I took the phone from him and followed him into the shop. "Hi, Martha, what's going on?"

"I just have a second, but I heard something a minute ago I thought you should know. Have you ever met Connie Minsker?"

"Sure, she's a stylist at Hair Apparent. What about her? She's not dead, too, is she?" I felt my stomach do a barrel roll as I thought about another body being discovered in Maple Ridge.

"Not that I know of. Why, what have you heard?"

"I haven't heard anything. You called me, remember?" I said, a little shorter than I should have. "Sorry, I'm a little on edge right now."

"You don't have to explain it to me. I was just at a Mommy Time session and I was beside Gracie Hawthorne on the mat. While our girls were playing, Gracie told me Connie was absolutely jubilant about Betty's murder."

Connie and I didn't have the same circle of friends, and I usually got my hair done in Emerson, but I knew her well enough to say hello to on the street. She was a brassy plat-

inum blonde with a size-fourteen figure she liked squeez-
ing into size-ten dresses.

"That's odd. Did Gracie have any idea why she would
be happy about it?"

"It was supposed to be some kind of confidence, but she
told Gracie that with Betty out of the way, she and Larry
could finally be together. She told her that with the alimony Larry was paying, he couldn't afford to get too serious with anybody else. According to Gracie, Connie
thinks that means she and Larry will be together now that
Betty's dead."

I hadn't eliminated any of my initial suspects, and my
friends were adding more! "I'll talk to her. Thanks for the
tip."

"You don't seem as enthusiastic as you were the other
night."

"No, I am. I really do appreciate it. Thank you."

"You're welcome. I'll call back if I hear anything else."

"You do that," I said.

David had been pretending to clean, but it was fairly obvious he'd been listening to every bit of my end of the conversation. "Am I going to get to follow up on any of these
leads you've been getting?"

"I don't know if that's such a good idea," I said. There
was no way I was going to put Hannah's son at risk. It was
one thing sticking my own neck out, but I couldn't let him
take any chances. Hannah would never forgive me if anything happened to David, and I wouldn't be able to forgive
myself, either.

"I'm perfectly capable of snooping around, too, you
know," David said.

"So, are you volunteering to go the beauty shop? I hear
a man went in there once in the seventies by accident, and

he never came out again. But if you want to get a haircut, be my guest."

His hand went to his ponytail. "I don't think so. I guess I'll pass on this one."

"Good enough. If you don't mind, I'm going to see if Connie can take me as a walk-in. Call if you need me here."

He looked around the empty shop. "There's not much chance of that, is there?"

I prepped my questions for Connie as I walked to Hair Apparent. The sun was trying to come out from behind a sheaf of clouds, and I could feel bursts of warmth when it managed to escape, but all in all, it was a gloomy, overcast day. It matched my mood perfectly: cloudy with brief bursts of hope.

The styling salon was on the back side of the brook walk, out of the high-dollar rent of the main stroll, and I was shivering a little by the time I got there.

After steeling myself for the interrogation to come, I put my hand on the doorknob. Then I heard a scream from inside.

Chapter 7

My instincts told me to run in the other direction, but like the fool I can sometimes be, I threw the door open instead. I was fully expecting to find bodies, blood, and a madman inside.

Instead, I saw Susan March clutching her hands to her head. Her hair was a shade of orange I'd never seen before, a startling contrast to the chestnut-tinted hue she usually favored.

"You've ruined my life," Susan screamed.

"It's not that bad," Connie said, her voice trying to soothe her distraught customer.

"Not that bad? I look like a carrot. A carrot that's on fire. What did you do to me?"

"You're the one who wanted a custom mix. How was I supposed to know your hair would react that way? Just sit back down in my chair. I can fix it."

I didn't see how, not without a set of shears and the keys to a wig factory.

Evidently Susan didn't either. "You're not touching my hair ever again," she screamed as she grabbed her coat and nearly knocked me off my feet as she raced by.

Connie didn't even seem disturbed by the scene. She brushed off her chair and said, "Next," but nobody would make eye contact with her, let alone risk her chair.

"I guess that's me," I said, gulping back my fear.

"Have a seat, Carolyn. Have you finally decided to let me get rid of that gray?"

I put a hand on my head to protect it, wondering what I'd gotten myself into. If my hair follicles could talk, they'd all be screaming bloody murder about now. "Just a light trim," I said. "Bill likes the gray."

As she put the smock around me, she said, "Now your husband's hair is a perfect example of how good gray can look. It's practically luminescent, isn't it? He always was a handsome man."

This conversation wasn't exactly going in the direction I wanted it to. "Thanks, I think so, too. I hear you have a new man in your life."

Her scissors paused in the air, and she pointed them at me like an accusing finger. "And where did you hear that?"

"You know how this town is. Word gets around."

She paused a moment, shrugged, then lowered her weapon. "I guess it doesn't matter anymore."

"What do you mean?" I asked as I watched the bobbing scissors. It probably hadn't been the best idea in the world, bracing a possible murderer when she had the means to commit another right there in her hands.

"I mean it's over. The rat dumped me this morning. Can you believe it? After all those promises. Lies, that's what they were. His alimony payments are gone now, so he decides to dump me for a younger model. I'm swearing off men, now and forever."

There are many women in the world who are perfectly fine without men in their lives, good and caring women who lead bountiful lives of blissful independence, but I knew Connie wasn't one of them. She needed a man like a fish needed water. She couldn't exist without them.

"I'm so sorry," I said, trying to sound sympathetic. "You must be devastated."

Connie's scissors paused again, and she lowered her head to mine as she said, "And after what I did for him, too. I still can't believe it."

"What did you do?" I asked. Was she about to confess her guilt to me?

"Things a proper lady doesn't talk about," she said after a moment's hesitation. "You know what I mean."

Honestly, I didn't have a clue. "Go on. It's all right. You can tell me."

For a moment, she moved around front and stared hard into my eyes. In a voice that was almost a whisper, she said, "No, actually, I can't."

A few seconds later, she pulled the smock off me and shook the few strands of hair she'd cut to the floor. "There you go. You look much better. That will be forty dollars."

I glanced in the mirror. Forty dollars, for that? She had to be kidding. When I looked back at her to challenge her pricing, I saw that she still held those scissors, poised like the weapon they could become. I didn't even grumble as I handed two folded twenties to her. Her free hand lingered in the air a moment, but the only tip she would get out of me was to leave town before a mob of angry women ran her out themselves. How on earth was I going to tell my husband I'd just frittered away forty dollars on a nearly nonexistent haircut? There was no way around it: I was going to have to make good the expenditure with my mad money, and boy, oh boy, had it earned its name this time.

At least my hair looked better than Susan March's had. She'd be wearing hats and scarves until she could find someone to fix her hair coloring. Taking that into consideration, I'd come out of it with the better deal.

Having seen the way Connie had handled Susan so calmly, almost dangerously still, I realized she might just be capable of committing a murder. I was in serious need of eliminating some of my suspects before all of Maple Ridge made my list.

I started back to Fire at Will, but then I remembered that check from Tamra Gentry in my purse. Knowing Tamra, I suspected she'd be calling Lynn Eckels, the principal of the elementary school, any time to ask about the progress of a fund-raiser that Lynn didn't even know the school was having. I just hoped the school could accept charitable donations for its book collections. I hated the idea of giving the money back when it could do so much good. I also hated the thought of having to explain my phony book fund to Tamra—not to mention Bill.

At least I had a relationship with Lynn. Her secretary showed me into her office as soon as I announced myself at the front desk.

"Carolyn, what a nice surprise. I just heard how much fun Miss Blackshire and her students had at your shop. I'm guessing you'll be getting two dozen thank-you notes by tomorrow."

"I was glad to do it."

"Come on in," she said as she waved me to a chair. Lynn had been an excellent teacher, and she'd moved up the ladder until she was running the place. They'd offered her the high school principal's job when Mr. Landingham finally retired, but she'd turned them down, preferring to stay with the younger children. I didn't blame her a bit. After she settled behind her desk, she said, "I know this isn't a social call, not in the middle of a workday. What can I do for you?"

"How's the library's supply of books for the students? Could you use any more?"

She nodded. "Always. I'm afraid our funding is rather light this year, but we can't accept used books. I'm sorry, it's school policy."

"I'm talking about new ones." I slid the check across the desk toward her. "I apologize if I shouldn't have done this. Feel free to scold me all you want."

She glanced at the check amount, then did a double take. "Are you sure you can afford it?"

"It's not my money," I said.

She looked back at the check and saw it was drawn on Tamra Gentry's account. "Okay, at least I don't have to ask if she can swing it." She looked at me a second, then asked, "Carolyn, what's this about? We're happy to take this donation, and I'll call to thank her as soon as you leave, but perhaps I should know how you happened to ask for the money in the first place."

I'd planned to come up with something to tell her that was close enough to the truth not to be an outright lie, but I couldn't bring myself to do it. "I was snooping into Betty Wickline's murder, and I made up the library book fund on the spot as a way to get my foot in the door."

She laughed vigorously for a few seconds, then quashed it. "You delight me, you know that?"

"Hey, it's the truth."

"I know, and how refreshing it is to hear it. Believe me, I've heard my share of whoppers sitting behind this desk. Thanks for that."

"Is the PTA going to be upset that I did this without their approval?"

"We don't have to tell them. I'll call Barbara Raskin, since she's running the show this year. By the time I get finished with her, she'll think it was her idea in the first place. Who knows, maybe you've started something here."

"Thanks, I knew I could count on you."

Lynn tapped the check with her finger. "Any time you need another ruse, feel free to raise more money for the school. We greatly appreciate it. Who knows? The PTA might even give you a plaque for this."

"Thanks, but tell them no thanks. Given the circumstances, I'd be too embarrassed to take it." I added two fifties, the one from Bill and another from me. Lynn looked at me curiously.

"Don't ask," was all I could say.

David was waiting on a customer when I got back to Fire at Will, a nice sight indeed. He nodded to me as he showed the young woman how to throw a pot on one of our electric pottery wheels. The scene always made me want to laugh. I'm a die-hard romantic, and I love the movie *Ghost* as much as any romantic—maybe more, since I deal with clay myself—but being behind the student wasn't all that practical as a teaching method, at least not as far as I was concerned. David, most sensibly, was sitting directly across from her, guiding her hands as she shaped the clay.

The front door chimed, and I wondered whether it was another customer or someone involved in my murder investigation. When I turned to face the door, I saw a young woman sporting stylish clothes and an elegant hairdo.

"May I help you?"

"I'd like some pot, please." She said the words softly, as if measuring them carefully before releasing them.

"Excuse me?" What exactly did she think "Fire at Will" meant?

"You know, some pot. Or some dish. Something to pretty." She was frowning at me like I'd lost my mind.

Okay, I caught the accent then. It was subtle, but it was still there. "You'd like to glaze a pot?"

"Yes, very much," she said as she nodded vigorously.

"Then let's have some fun."

By the time she'd finished decorating one of our largest pots with flourishes of flowers, Ekaterina and I had become fast friends. "When ready?" she asked as she took off the smock I'd given here.

"Give us four days," I said as I held up four fingers.

"Good." After she paid me with a hundred from a large stack that I happened to glimpse in her purse, Ekaterina left the shop smiling. I was hoping she'd come again soon, and not just because she could afford anything I had in the shop. Her enthusiasm was contagious, and I'd enjoyed showing her how to transform plain bisque-fired clay into what I was certain would be a work of art.

David wasn't having as much luck with his student as I'd had with mine. I heard her say, "I just can't do this. It doesn't look anything like yours."

In a calming voice, he said, "You need to be patient. It takes time to master throwing pots."

"But it's so messy," the woman protested.

I heard David sigh. "Yes, wet clay and liquid slip can get a little dirty. Maybe you'd like to try your hand at glazing? It might be a good first step."

"No, I'm going to learn how to do this. But not today. Yuck, I'm a mess."

As she scrubbed her hands in one of our sinks, David

shot me a look that didn't need much interpretation. His student was barely out the door when he asked, "Can you believe that? She didn't want to get dirty! Where did she think she was, a nail salon?"

"She paid, didn't she?"

David nodded angrily. "With fifty-cent pieces! Can you believe it? She had a whole purse full of them."

"They're still legal tender. At least she covered her bill."

"How about your customer? Did she pay you in euros?"

I grinned. "Wasn't her accent adorable? No, she had a stack of hundreds in her purse."

I was feeling good about the world again. Ekaterina had had that effect on me. The warm glow died instantly when the sheriff stormed into my shop.

"What did you say to my wife?"

So it was going to be one of those conversations. Well, if the sheriff was looking for a fight, he'd come to the right place.

"I didn't say anything to her that is any of your business," I snapped back, matching his tone.

"You shouldn't have talked to her."

I saw David edging toward the back, and a part of me didn't blame him. This wasn't his fight, at least not this part of it.

"She nearly ran me down on the sidewalk outside my shop. What was I supposed to do, just ignore her?"

He huffed a few times, as if trying to catch his breath. "I'm not talking about that, and you know it. Why did you bring up Betty Wickline's name?"

"We were standing out in front after a murder happened here. What did you want me to do, ask her about the weather?" I took a deep breath myself and added, "She reacted rather strongly to Betty's name."

"They never did get along," he answered sullenly.

"If you ask me, I think your wife is glad Betty's dead."

Okay, maybe I was pushing him a little too hard, but I wanted to see his reaction. I'd been hoping for a screaming denial, or at least some response. Instead, I saw his expression go as cold as ice. Two seconds later, he stormed out without another word.

David poked his nose around the corner. "Is it safe to come out?"

"I don't know, but the sheriff's gone, if that's what you're asking."

He shook his head. "Wow. You really know how to get along with law enforcement, don't you, Carolyn? I thought for a second there he was going to shoot you."

"It wouldn't have surprised me a bit," I admitted as I started to shake. Confrontation always did that to me, and though I never backed down, I wasn't always that comfortable arguing with anybody but my husband. "He reacted pretty forcefully, didn't he? What do you think that means?"

"I think it means he was defending his wife," David said.

"Does that mean you think she needs to be defended?"

"Don't read too much into it," he said. "To be honest with you, I kind of admire the guy for doing it."

"Maybe," I said. Was David right in his assumption that Hodges was just being overprotective of his wife, or was the sheriff hiding something darker and more sinister? I didn't know yet, but I wasn't finished pushing him, either. If my prying made some folks around town mad at me, they were just going to have to learn to live with it. I wasn't about to go to jail for a murder I didn't commit.

• • •

"That was a truly great day," David said as we stood on the sidewalk and locked the store up at closing time. "It was nice having actual customers in the shop again."

"I could get used to it myself," I said with a grin. The bite of my earlier conversation with Sheriff Hodges was gone, probably because I'd been doing what I loved for most of the afternoon. "Do you have big plans this evening?"

"I've got a class tonight on Renaissance art. It's all I can do to stay awake in it."

"I'd love to hear that lecture. You're so lucky."

"Want to trade evenings? I'm sure whatever you're doing will be more exciting than my plans."

I patted his shoulder. "I'm not sure Bill would enjoy your cooking."

"Hey, I'm a good cook. I make a mean waffle. Ask Mom."

"Between the two of you, you've got breakfast just about covered then."

"So what else is on tap for your evening?" he asked.

"I don't know. After that, we might play some Scrabble, or maybe watch an old movie. There's a Don Knotts retrospective on tonight, and I'm dying to see *The Ghost and Mister Chicken* again."

"Art class it is, then." He shrugged, then added, "See you later, Carolyn."

"Bye, David."

Despite the impression I'd just given my assistant, I didn't have to get home right away. Bill had warned me earlier in the day that he was going to be working late for the next few days finishing up a pair of Shaker dressers a customer had ordered. Since I wasn't cooking dinner, there was no real need to go straight home. Despite the sheriff's desire that I butt out of the murder investigation, I was going to push forward and shake a few more trees to see what might fall out.

"Carolyn, over here."

Kendra Williams called out to me as I walked by her place. Had she been lying in wait for me to pass by? A part of me regretted that she wasn't terrified of me anymore. At least then I might have gotten some peace and quiet. But then again, maybe she had more on Betty Wickline's love life, and I needed all the help I could get tracking down her latest paramour.

I paused for a second, then turned toward her. "Were you calling me?" I asked. "I was deep in thought."

As I approached her, she asked, "Were you thinking about the murder?"

"Among other things," I said. "Do you have anything new for me?"

"About Betty's latest love? No, nothing yet. I was just wondering if you've managed to uncover any more clues." The woman was positively salivating at the prospect of hearing more dirt on the murder victim. No matter how I'd felt about Betty—and let's face it, the whole world knew my feelings—I wasn't about to drag her name through the dirt any more than I had to.

"I'm still working on it," I said.

I was trying to find a delicate way to disengage from her when Kendra said, "You should talk to Annie Gregg."

"I don't believe I know her," I said.

"She's Don Gregg's daughter."

"Still no bells," I said.

"From Harvest Glenn," she continued.

"Okay, I know where the town is, but I still don't know the Greggs. What do they have to do with Betty?"

Kendra looked disgusted. "Not Don, he's an engineer

for the county, and as far as I know, he never even met Betty Wickline."

"So why should I speak with his daughter?"

"You really don't have a clue, do you? Annie cleans houses all around the county. She's saving up to go to school, since Don's paying alimony from his first marriage and doesn't have a dime to spare."

This woman was driving me crazy. In fact, if Kendra's body was ever found in her shop, I wouldn't have any problem being named a suspect in that particular crime.

"And that matters how?" I asked.

"She cleaned Betty Wickline's house." Kendra lowered her voice as she added, "Not only does she have the dirt on Betty, and I mean that literally, but she's also got something much more important. She has a key to Betty's house."

That certainly got my attention. "How do I get in touch with her?"

Kendra handed me a slip of paper. "That's her cellphone number. Give her a call, Carolyn."

"I will. And Kendra?"

"What?"

"Thanks."

She looked startled by my appreciation, and if I didn't know any better, I could swear she blushed slightly for just a second. "You're welcome." She looked down the walk, then asked eagerly, "Any chance I could go with you when you search the house? I might be able to find something you would miss. I've got a keen eye for detail, you know."

And just when I was starting to feel all warm and fuzzy toward her. "No, thanks, I can handle it."

"You *will* tell me what you find though, won't you?"

It was probably the least I could do, given that she'd handed me this lead herself. "Fine. I'll let you know."

I was tempted to call Annie on the spot, but I needed some privacy for the conversation, and some kind of plan to get her to open up to me without alerting her to my true intentions. Blast it all, I suddenly realized that I was walking toward the upper parking lot when I'd parked my car in the opposite direction. I had to walk past Kendra's shop again to get to where I'd left the Intrigue early that morning, but Kendra was busy haggling with a customer, so I made it past her the second time unscathed.

Back at my home, I raced around the house tidying up before Annie Gregg showed up for our appointment. She'd readily agreed to come for an interview. I didn't need someone to clean up after my husband and me, but it was the only way I could think of to get some time with the girl. My, how had the place gotten so dusty? I ran a rag over the high spots, stopping long enough to put away a few errant things like last week's laundry and some magazines from the Carter administration. I just about had the place in good order when the doorbell rang.

I opened the door to find a trim, young brunette with big brown eyes waiting for me. She reminded me of someone, but I couldn't put my finger on who.

"You must be Annie," I said as I offered her my hand.

"And you're Mrs. Emerson."

"It's Carolyn, please," I said. "Won't you come in?"

"Thanks."

As I took her coat, I could see Annie studying the place. I glanced around, unsure of what she was seeing. After all, I'd cleaned up, hadn't I? I had to admit, there were some spots my dust rag had missed, and the magazines I'd so carefully stacked by the sofa in the living room had fallen over like a house of cards.

"Can I get you something to drink? Some coffee, or perhaps a cup of tea?"

"If it's not too much trouble, I'd love some tea."

"Then why don't you come back into the kitchen and we can chat there?"

I saw a few things I'd missed in there as well. Maybe after my investigation was over, I'd consider hiring Annie after all. It might be nice to have an extra hand sometimes, since Bill wasn't about to pitch in. That wasn't entirely fair; he'd help out whenever I asked, but it would be lovely not having to ask.

As Annie settled onto a bar stool, she said, "I have Wednesday mornings and Thursday afternoons free, but I'm afraid I'm booked solid the rest of the week."

"My, you're an ambitious young lady, aren't you?"

She shrugged. "I want to go to Stanford, and at the rate I'm working and saving, I'll be able to register next year."

"That's a difficult school to get into, isn't it?" As soon as the words left my mouth I realized I sounded a bit snobbish. "It doesn't mean I don't think you aren't qualified. Oh dear, I've really stepped in it, haven't I?"

Instead of being angry, Annie just laughed. "Don't worry, it's pretty hard to offend me. I got in on my own, and I'm planning to use student loans if I have to, but I'm hoping to get a partial scholarship to supplement the earnings I've made cleaning."

"Then I probably can't afford you," I said as the kettle started to whistle.

"Don't be so sure. It's not as bad as you might think."

She quoted me a price that would take my entire "fun fund" from Bill's chair earnings as well as a nice chunk out of my weekly house budget. It appeared that I was going to have to make do on my own, at least until I had a chain of Fire at Will shops instead of my lone store.

As we sipped our tea, I said, "I understand you worked for Betty Wickline."

Her mug paused midway between the counter and her lips. "That was a terrible thing, wasn't it? That's why I have Thursday afternoons free." She hesitated a second, then asked, "They found her in your shop, didn't they?"

"I didn't kill her," I said bluntly, wondering how many times I'd have to make that particular declaration.

"Why, I never thought you did," she said. "If we're being honest, maybe it did cross my mind a few times. It looks bad for you, doesn't it, Carolyn?"

"That's the problem," I said. "There are enough folks who could cripple my business with a boycott if I don't figure out what really happened to Betty. Is there anything you might have seen or heard that might help me?"

She frowned. "What about the sheriff? Surely he's investigating the crime."

I shook my head. "I've got reason to believe he might be involved in it himself."

Annie took a sip of tea, then said, "That's a pretty bold accusation."

"I've got my reasons, but I'd rather not tell you what they are. Annie, I'm in trouble. Will you help me?"

She looked startled by the request, then said, "I wish I could, but I'm not sure what I can do. I just clean; I don't snoop when I'm doing it."

"I never meant to imply that you did," I said. There was something about this girl I liked. She was forthright and open with her emotions, and as far as I could tell, guileless. "I'm just wondering if you might have seen or heard anything that made you suspicious."

After pondering my question for a minute, she replied, "No, sorry, there's nothing I can think of."

"Do you still have a key to her place?" I'd debated asking her, but really, what choice did I have?

"Yes," she said softly. "Why do you ask?"

"Maybe if we could go over there together, I could look around some. I don't want to disturb her things, but there might be something there that might tell me who killed her."

I doubted she could have looked more uncomfortable. "I don't know about this, Carolyn. It seems kind of sneaky."

"That's because it is," I agreed. "Forget it. I shouldn't have asked. I didn't mean to put you in an awkward position. How's your tea?"

"It's fine," she said. After a full minute of silence, Annie said, "I do have some of my things over there I need to get. Some cleaning supplies and things like that. I suppose you could go with me."

"I don't want you to do anything you're not comfortable with," I said, trying to hide my elation.

"No, it's okay. I can't imagine how horrible it must be to be suspected of murder and not be able to do anything about it."

"You're a real sweetheart," I said as I patted her hand.

"When would you like to go?"

"How about right now? Let me grab my car keys and I'll follow you there."

"Okay, I guess that would be all right."

The poor girl barely knew what hit her. I was afraid if I gave her any time at all to think about what she was doing, she'd back out, no matter how sympathetic she was to my cause. And I couldn't afford that. I had to ratchet up my efforts if I was going to find Betty Wickline's killer, and if that meant crossing a line with the sheriff, then I was going to walk boldly across it. As I followed her through town toward Betty's place, I kept hoping that Annie wouldn't get cold feet and bar my access after all.

To my relief, she led me around the drive to the back of the house, and after we both parked, she got out and said, "I always had to park back here. It's the only lock my key fits."

It was a rather modest home, not quite what I'd been expecting. A thought suddenly occurred to me. How had Betty afforded Annie's services? Where was her money coming from? As we approached the door, I wondered what we were going to find inside.

Chapter 8

"Oh, my lands, what happened here?"

I followed Annie inside and looked around the kitchen. We'd turned on one of the lights, and I hoped no one saw us snooping.

The kitchen was a wreck. The contents of cereal boxes, flour bins, coffee tins, and other containers had been strewn out across the counters. Not a drawer or door was left unopened, and the remnants of Betty Wickline's pantry looked like a hurricane had hit it.

"I'm guessing it wasn't like this the last time you saw it," I said.

"Of course not."

Annie started cleaning up when I put a hand on her arm. "You probably shouldn't do that. The police are going to want to see this before we touch anything."

"You're right. I wasn't thinking. My first reaction to a mess is to clean it up, do you know what I mean?"

"For now, you'd better resist the urge," I said.

Annie reached for Betty's phone when I stopped her. "We shouldn't touch anything, remember?"

"I keep forgetting. Let me get my cell phone."

As she dug into her purse, I asked, "What for?"

She looked at me, the confusion clear in her eyes. "We're going to call the police and report this, remember?"

"Not just yet," I said. "Why don't we look around a little first?" There was no way Hodges was going to let me search the place after he was on the scene, and really, what did it matter if I called him right now, or in half an hour?

"I don't know about this, Carolyn," Annie said. "This is a little more than I bargained for."

"You can leave if you want to. I'll say the back door was open, and I saw a light on or something like that. I won't even tell the police you were with me."

Annie shook her head, looked around a second, then said, "No, I'm fine. I'll stay here with you."

"You really don't have to."

"I'm not going to leave you with another mess on your hands," she said. Then she looked around again. "I didn't mean this."

"I knew what you meant, and I appreciate it. Try not to step in the spilled flour. We don't want to leave any footprints."

I know Annie was right. We should have called Hodges right away—and I was going to call him eventually, honestly I was—but I needed to have a look around first.

"You go ahead," Annie said. "I'm going to sit right here." Her look was full of pleading as she added, "Don't be long, Carolyn, okay?"

"I promise I'll make it quick."

I carefully skirted the spilled flour and made my way deeper into the house. Whoever had trashed the place hadn't stopped at the kitchen. Sofa cushions had been slashed open in the living room, and the master suite was even worse. The mattress and box spring were on the floor, with cuts across the fabric. Entire drawers were pulled out of the dressers and their contents added to the pile. What had the mysterious visitor been looking for? Betty must have been keeping some kind of secret, but what could it have been? I walked into the closet and felt more than a tick of envy as I surveyed an unbelievably large space. That's when I realized she had converted one of the bedrooms into a closet. This woman must have had a budget for shoes that was more than my mortgage payment. It was just one more indication that Betty Wickline had a source of income that nobody else knew about.

"Carolyn, are you finished? I'm getting nervous."

"I won't be much longer," I called out. I was about to give up on the closet when I noticed something poking out from the toe of one of the shoes. It was a key, like the kind for lockers at the Y or at a bus terminal. But what could it mean? I tucked it into my purse and started rooting around the other shoes when I heard a voice behind me.

"Stand up slowly, and don't make a move."

"How can I stand if I can't move?" I asked.

There was no mistaking the voice. It was our town sheriff, and from the sound of it, he was ready to shoot me first and ask questions later.

When I turned around, he had his gun out of his holster, but at least it was by his side instead of pointing at me. I said, "You can put that away. I'm not dangerous, you know."

"I'm not so sure. What do you think you're doing here?"

It was time to dance. "I came by with Annie to get her cleaning supplies, and while she was in the kitchen, I thought I heard a kitten mewing back here. What did you want me to do, leave the poor thing here to die?"

He looked around the closet. "I don't see any cats."

I did my best to look perplexed. "Funny, I don't either, now that you mention it. It must have been the wind."

"It's dead calm outside."

Okay, he wasn't buying it, but I didn't exactly have a fallback position. "Sure it is right now, but what about five minutes ago? Or have you been out there waiting for me to make a break for it?"

"I just got here," he admitted.

"Well, there you go." At least he couldn't dispute my claim of a gust of wind sounding like a kitten, no matter how much he wanted to. "What brings you here?"

"A neighbor saw a light on and called us. Tell me you didn't trash this place, Carolyn."

The mere thought of creating such mess and mayhem shook me. "Now why on earth would I do that?"

"That's exactly what I'm asking."

"We found it like this. Every bit of it," I said, my right-eous indignation valid for once. "Ask Annie."

"I did," he agreed reluctantly. "That doesn't mean you didn't come back after you'd already wrecked the place once."

"If I had a key, why would I have needed Annie?" I wasn't sure if I had just made an admission in there some-place, but I didn't want the sheriff to have time to think about it. "This proves that someone else murdered Betty. Don't you see that?"

"I'm listening."

"Well, I didn't do it. Why would I come back here if I'd done this? Whoever did it was looking for something, and from the state of things, I'm guessing he didn't find it."

Hodges nodded. "So that's why you came back. You

brought Annie this time as a cover in case I showed up, which was actually pretty clever of you, because here I am."

"I didn't do this," I said, nearly in tears despite my resolve to keep my head. Why wouldn't the man believe me?

"I'm not willing to say what I think yet one way or the other," he said, but at least he put his gun back in its holster. "There's another theory you haven't brought up yet, one that might be closer to the truth."

"What's that? If you've got an explanation, I'm ready to hear it."

He gestured around the bedroom. "This might not be related to Betty Wickline's murder at all, at least not in the way you think it is."

"Now who's stretching for something?" I asked.

"There have been a string of burglaries in Hartford that this MO matches. The crooks read the obituaries, then scout the houses of the deceased. This fits that pattern."

I pointed to the mattress, which I could see a corner of from my vantage point in the closet. "So why rip up the box frame?"

"How should I know? Would you like me to go back to my original theory that you were here snooping around for something Betty Wickline had on you?"

"No, I can see how the burglary theory is possible," I said, backpedaling as fast as I could.

"I thought you might. Come on, let's get out of here."

"Aren't you at least going to dust the place for fingerprints?" I asked.

"I've got a feeling all we'll find are yours and Betty Wickline's," he said. "Even if you're telling the truth, which I'm not about to admit, you should have called me before you started exploring on your own. Annie had the right idea. She was sitting on a bar stool by the door when

I walked in. She nearly fainted when she saw my drawn gun."

"Okay, maybe I should have called you, but would you have believed my story any more if I'd reported this before I had a look around myself?"

"What happened to the cat?"

For a split second, I almost said, "What cat?" but providence stopped me. "That's what I just said. I was looking for the cat."

"Sure you were," he said as he started toward the front door of the house.

"We came in the back way," I said.

"And you're leaving through here." He unlocked the door and opened it. "Stay away from this place, Carolyn. I'll lock you up if I have to."

"I'd really rather you didn't," I said.

Annie was gone when I got outside, and I honestly couldn't blame her. Even if I could afford her cleaning tab, I doubted she'd be willing to work for me anymore. As I walked around the outside of the house back to the Intrigue, I realized that something was stuck to the bottom of one of my shoes. It was the torn third of a piece of paper, and when I turned it over, I saw the letters "is," and just below it "ight." Underneath that was "one". What on earth could that mean? I thought about sharing my discovery with the sheriff, but after our conversation, I wasn't in any mood to go back for more lecturing. I tucked the paper into my purse along with the key and wondered what they meant.

I was tired, and my confrontation with the sheriff had taken more out of me than I'd realized. Though I probably should have done some more investigating, all I wanted was a quiet bite and a long bath. It was probably just as well that Bill was working on those dressers. I wasn't in the mood for company, not even his.

That's why it surprised me so much when I saw the lights on in our house when I drove up.

My dear husband was sitting on the sofa, and from the look on his face, he'd had a day nearly as bad as mine.

"I thought you were working late," I said. I put my jacket on the armchair. "I'd be glad to whip something up for you to eat, if you'd like."

"I already ate," he said. "Carolyn, this has gotten out of hand."

"What are you talking about?"

"The sheriff called me a few minutes ago and told me what happened. What were you thinking, walking around Betty Wickline's place like you held the deed? Are you trying to get arrested?"

"I've had enough lectures for today, thank you very much." The nerve of the man! He was actually scolding me.

"That's too bad, because you're listening to one more. Stay out of this, Carolyn."

"What makes you think you have any right to tell me what to do? Has that ever worked for you in the past?"

I was expecting another lashing, but instead, his scowl broke into a grin. "Now that you mention it, not that I can recall."

"So what makes you think it will work now?" I wasn't ready to forgive him, no matter how adorable he looked at the moment.

"I don't guess I do," he said as he rubbed a hand through his hair. I knew from years of marriage that that sign meant he was perplexed about the situation, and that he was giving up. That was one of the nicest things about being married to the same person for so long: after enough practice, you could read your spouse's body language almost better than the newspaper.

"Just be careful," he said softly.

"I will, but I can't give up now." I thought about sharing my finds with him, but I knew I shouldn't push it. "Now that you've scolded me, you can go back to work."

"To tell you the truth, I'd rather hang around here with you, if that's okay."

"No more lectures?" I asked, raising one eyebrow as I stared at him.

"I can't promise that," he said slightly.

"I know." I hugged my husband a little harder and longer than usual, drawing strength from him. I always felt safest in his arms, and I needed that more than anything at the moment.

"Hey, are you all right?" he whispered softly into my ear.

I pulled away. "I am now. I'm going to make myself an omelet. Are you sure you wouldn't like some?"

"I could probably eat a bite, just to keep you company."

The old bear ended up eating more than I did, but I didn't mind. I'd had a feeling he would, so I had adjusted the portions accordingly.

After we'd eaten, he said, "Tell you what, why don't you go grab that bath, and I'll do the dishes." He rarely made such an offer, so I knew Bill was really worried about me.

"I think I'll take you up on that," I said, and went straight to the bathroom before he had a chance to change his mind. By the time I got out of the tub, he was on the couch, a book propped up on his belly, though his eyes were closed and he was softly snoring.

"Come on, you old bear. It's time for bed."

"I wasn't sleeping," he protested drowsily.

"Sure you weren't. I'm going to bed. Coming?"

He rubbed his eyes. "I'm right behind you."

The next morning, the telephone at Fire at Will was ringing as I walked in the door. "Carolyn, I'm glad I caught you. I just found out something you should know about Betty Wickline."

"Good morning to you, too, Martha."

"Sorry, I didn't mean to be so abrupt. We're going to my mother-in-law's for a week, and I wanted to catch you before we left home."

"You poor dear. I'm so sorry." Bill's mother had been the queen of passive-aggressive behavior, and it had taken me the first ten years of our marriage to undue the damage that the woman had inflicted on my husband. She'd been a nightmare all the way around. The best thing that had ever happened to our marriage was when Gert had moved to Canada. Everyone else was flocking to Florida as they hit their retirement years, but not Bill's mother. It figured she would go against the norm.

"Are you kidding? Stella's wonderful. She takes the kids for a few hours a day and plans a special treat for me on our visits. Last year she got me an hour with a masseuse, and this year she's promised a full spa treatment. To be honest with you, I won the lottery when I married Charlie."

"Then strike what I said before. I'm happy for you. So, tell me this news."

She lowered her voice and said, "A friend of mine named Myrna Stout saw Betty the night she was murdered. She was having an argument on the street near your shop."

I knew Myrna. She had run Crazy Quilts until her degenerating eyesight had forced her to sell the business. I wasn't sure what kind of eyewitness Myrna would make if she was ever called to testify. "Why are you whispering?"

"Charlie's in the next room packing, and I don't want him to hear me. He's not that thrilled with my snooping."

"Neither is Bill," I admitted. "I don't want to get you in trouble with your husband."

"Don't worry about that. I can handle him. The only problem is, Myrna didn't know the man Betty was arguing with. She said she didn't recognize him, but we both know what that probably means."

"I'm guessing she didn't give you any kind of description."

"Sorry, she said it was dark. I guess it wasn't as big a tip as I thought."

"You never know. Thanks for calling."

I could hear her husband calling, "Martha, where are my golf shoes? I know they're in here somewhere."

"They're in the garage next to your clubs," Martha said. To me, she added, "Carolyn, I've got to go. Packing for this family for a week is like moving the army."

"Bye, and have fun."

"You bet. Bye."

I wondered about the identity of the man Betty had been arguing with. Could it have been the sheriff? It was possible. Myrna had lived in town all her life, but would she know Hodges's voice from a distance? Or Larry Wickline's, for that matter? Who else could it have been? Herman had a key so he had to be on my list, but would Myrna have recognized him in the dark, either? I doubted the two of them traveled in the same circles. Could it have been Robert Owens, perhaps? The potter was new to Maple Ridge. But he'd claimed to be out of town, back in North Carolina. Besides, surely she'd be able to recognize his southern accent. Or did he have it when he was shouting?

I didn't know, and I wasn't going to get into an argument with him just to test my theory. I wasn't sure how I could check his alibi, and I wondered if I should tell the sheriff. Then I realized something else. Did that eliminate my female suspects? I had a handful of those as well, and it would certainly help my investigation if I could pare my list in half. That way I could drop Tamra Gentry, Connie Minsker, Evelyn Hodges, and even Kendra Williams, along with the rest of the female population of Maple Ridge.

Then again, maybe the argument didn't have anything to do with Betty's murder. Detecting was harder than it looked—there was no doubt about that—but I had no choice.

Jenna came in the shop a few minutes after I opened. Usually I welcomed any of the members of the Firing Squad, but from the dour expression on her face, I was afraid this wasn't about the latest glaze we were trying at the shop.

"We need to talk," she said.

"Those words usually strike terror in the hearts of married men, but to be honest with you, I'm not too keen on them right now myself. What's going on?"

"The whispers are growing," she said.

"Don't tell me. I'm being tried in the court of public opinion, aren't I?"

"The longer this case goes unsolved, the more folks are starting to believe you might have had something to do with Betty's murder. Have you made any progress?"

"Not that you'd notice. I keep adding suspects instead of eliminating them. It's growing at a pretty scary rate. I'm beginning to wonder if the woman had any friends at all. If she did, I haven't been able to find them."

"I'm surprised you didn't stumble across anything at

her house last night. Carolyn Emerson, what were you thinking? I can't believe the sheriff caught you breaking and entering."

"We had a key," I said, though even I realized how feeble I sounded.

"You had someone with you? Would you care to name your co-conspirator?"

"So how is it that everyone knows I was there, but not the identity of my accomplice?"

She didn't take the bait. "So you admit it's true?"

"I had a legitimate purpose for being there," I said.

"I'd love to hear it." Jenna gave me a stern look that must have intimidated attorneys on both sides, but she wasn't a judge anymore, and we weren't in court.

"I'm sorry, I'm starting to forget again. Whose side are you on?"

She frowned. "I believe you—you shouldn't even have to ask—but you have to consider how this looks to everyone else."

"And here I thought I was trying to solve a murder instead of being elected maple-syrup queen."

"It's obvious I can't talk to you when you're like this," she said. "We'll discuss it later."

"Or we won't," I said without even looking at her. I wasn't a big fan of being lectured to, not by Jenna, not by Bill, not by anybody.

I looked down at the sales catalog of glazes I'd been reading when Jenna had come in. I expected to hear her leave, but after a few seconds, when there wasn't a whisper of movement in the store, I looked up and saw tears tracking down her cheeks. All thoughts of my indignation were swept away in that trickle as I dropped the catalog and hugged my friend.

"I'm sorry. I shouldn't have snapped at you like that," I said.

Jenna shook her head as she pulled away. "I'm the one who owes you an apology. Sometimes it's hard to remember that I'm not a judge anymore. I have a tendency to overstep my bounds. It's just because I care about you, Carolyn."

"I care about you, too," I said. "And I really do appreciate your input."

"But you'll do as you wish anyway, is that it?"

I shrugged. "I don't have much choice." I thought about sharing the clues I'd found at Betty's house the night before, but I suddenly realized I should be talking to the entire group about it. And that included David, no matter how Hannah felt about it. I needed to gather them together to discuss where things stood, but I couldn't do it in the evening. With Martha out of town, that left Jenna, Butch, David, and Sandy. Sandy was the only one with regular employment, and if she couldn't make it, I could catch her up later. "We need to have a meeting," I said.

"I'm ready if you are. What would you like to talk about?"

"Not just the two of us," I said. "You call Butch and I'll call Sandy. David's due in here in half an hour, so let's make it then. Sorry, I should have asked. Are you free this morning?"

"I'm all yours, and I'd be delighted to help in any way I can. I should have said that the second I walked in the door instead of coming here to scold you."

"Is that what that was? I didn't notice," I said with a grin. "Call Butch."

I knew the reformed crook would come at Jenna's bidding, and David wouldn't be a problem. I dialed Sandy's number at the library. After I identified myself, I said,

"Hey, is there any way you could come over to the shop in half an hour? We're going to have a special meeting of the Firing Squad."

"I don't know. Things are kind of crazy around here. What happened? Did you get a new kiln or something?"

"No, I guess I should have explained. It's about Betty Wickline."

There was a long pause, so before she could answer, I added, "It's okay with me if you can't make it. I understand. I'll bring you up to date after we meet."

"Let me talk to Corki and I'll get back to you." Corki Mills was the library director in our town, and she'd come by the shop to try her hand at some glazing a few times in the past. We shared the same love of books and had spent a few pleasant Saturdays discussing the latest bestsellers.

"Okay, come by if you can, but seriously, don't worry if you can't."

After I hung up, Jenna said, "Butch is busy, but he's going to try to get here."

"What's he doing? Did he say?"

"No." Jenna frowned. "He was a little too reticent for my taste. I do hope he hasn't slipped."

"I'm sure he hasn't," I said, though I wished I felt as positive as I tried to sound. It would break Jenna's heart to see Butch back behind bars. I wondered if romance was beginning to blossom there, and how they would deal with such disparate pasts. Love had found stranger places to grow, though.

"What do we do in the meantime?"

I opened the cash register and pulled out a twenty. "Would you mind getting us some coffee and maybe something to nibble on? I hate to ask, but I can't leave the shop. Our coffeepot died last week, and I haven't gotten around to replacing it yet." It wasn't the greatest choice of words, but she knew what I meant.

"I'd be delighted, but you should keep your money. This will be my treat."

I kept the twenty extended in my hand. "I insist."

"But I want to."

I laughed at her, then said, "Jenna, we can stand here trying to out-stubborn each other until everybody else arrives, but then we won't have anything to offer the rest of our group, will we?"

She took the twenty, then paused at the door. "Just because I took your money doesn't mean I'm going to use it."

And then she ducked out before I could reply.

I didn't fritter away my time while I waited for the others to arrive. For once, I was glad for our lack of customers. It gave me time to set things up in the back of the shop. When the group started trickling in twenty minutes later, I'd set up a blackboard we used sometimes for teaching and had the chairs arranged in back. Hopefully the Firing Squad would have some insights into the information I'd acquired. Without their help, I didn't stand a chance of figuring out who had killed Betty Wickline, and why.

Chapter 9

Butch glanced at his watch after David showed up and Jenna returned with coffees and pastries. "Can we get this moving? I've got something going on I can't leave for too long at a time."

"Would you care to share what that might be with the rest of us?" Jenna asked.

"No, ma'am, I'm playing this one close to the vest."

I looked at the clock and saw that it was time to start. "Sandy must not have been able to get away. That's fine. I'll call her after we finish."

I dead-bolted the front door and flipped the sign to "Closed." David said, "This must be serious if you're willing to turn away paying customers."

"We can't very well have them barging in on us, can we? Let's all go to the back."

We walked back together and three seconds later heard a pounding on the front door.

"Should I see who it is?" David asked.

"No, they'll just have to come back later." I was serious about figuring this out, and if it meant I lost some sales in the short run, so be it.

Ten seconds later my store phone rang. "Let the machine get it," I told David as he reached for it.

Then my cell phone rang. What was going on? It had been quiet all morning, and now I couldn't get a moment's peace. I flipped it open and said, "Hello?"

"Hey, it's Sandy. I've been pounding on the front door. Didn't you hear me?"

"Hang on a second." I hung up the phone and walked to the front. As I let Sandy in, she said, "I thought you'd all gone somewhere else."

"Sorry, I didn't want to let any customers in."

"No, you can't have that, can you? Corki's covering the desk. She said she felt like she was on her old turf again. She had my job before I got it. You knew that, didn't you?"

"That's what she told me one day. We're all in back," I said as we joined the others.

"Where's Martha?" Sandy asked. "What a silly question. With that clan of hers, I'm always amazed when she makes our regular meetings."

"She's out of town," I said. "Shall we get started?"

Sandy said, "I suppose you're all wondering why I've gathered you here today. Sorry, I've always wanted to say that."

I shook my head, fighting to hide my smile. I couldn't afford any merriment. Things were getting dire.

"Okay, thanks for coming everyone. I need your help again. I've been collecting information, but so far, I haven't been able to figure out what to do with it."

Butch said, "I always make lists when I'm trying to decide something tough. Good points and bad, you know?"

"That's what I do as well," Jenna said.

"Thus the blackboard," I said. "I'm going to list the suspects I've got so far, and I need your help figuring out what I should do next."

"Write on," Sandy said. "Sorry, it makes more sense if you see it in print." She took the chalk from me and wrote "Right On" and beside it, "Write On."

I erased it, then said, "My, you're in a good mood."

"I'm sorry, I know this is serious, but Jake asked me out again today, and he sent me half a dozen red roses at work."

"How sweet," Jenna said.

"Why didn't he spring for a whole dozen?" Butch asked. "What is he, cheap?"

"Please, can we focus here?" Honestly, sometimes I felt like I was herding cats.

Everyone murmured apologies and then fell silent. I wrote the names of my suspects on the board down the left side, and it was an impressive list by the time I was finished. It read:

> *Sheriff Hodges*
> *Evelyn Hodges*
> *Larry Wickline*
> *Robert Owens*
> *Herman Meadows*
> *Tamra Gentry*
> *Connie Minsker*
> *Kendra Williams*

Butch whistled as I finished. "That's quite a roll call. A few of the names I'm not sure about. Care to explain how they made your roster? Some motives might be nice."

I nodded. After all, it was a fair question. "The sheriff may or may not have been having an affair with Betty, and Larry Wickline could have been trying to get out of paying any more alimony. I'm not sure about Robert Owens, but he admitted knowing her, and he has a key. The same goes for Herman Meadows."

"And exactly who is he again?" Jenna asked.

"Sorry. He's my landlord. He also owns a few other places along the brook walk." I turned back to the board. "Let's see, Betty was on Tamra's hung jury, and there's a suspicion Betty might have been blackmailing her." I glanced for a split second at Jenna, who studiously avoided my gaze. "Connie Minsker wanted to marry Larry Wickline, but he kept refusing, claiming alimony payments as his excuse. By the way, if Connie did kill Betty, Larry better watch his back. He dumped her after the murder, and Connie's ready to skin him alive."

Sandy asked, "Now how on earth did you know that?"

"I was getting a trim, and Connie told me."

She studied my hair. "It doesn't look any different to me. Were you at the beauty shop for a styling or for some snooping?"

"Both," I said.

David added, "Can we get back to your list? I understand Evelyn Hodges being on it, but why Kendra? The woman drives me crazy most of the time, but that doesn't make her a murderer."

"She had a key to the shop, and despite what Herman Meadows thinks, I'm positive I locked up that night. Well, almost positive. Fairly certain, anyway."

Butch smiled. "So you might have forgotten to lock the place up."

"It's a possibility," I admitted. "It's happened a few times before."

Butch shook his head. "Carolyn, you need to shut the place up tight every night. There are dangerous people out there."

I resisted any pot-and-kettle analogies. "I've been careful ever since. So, there you have it."

Jenna spoke up. "Don't forget the last leg of the tripod. The murderer needed the opportunity to commit the crime. Can you rule any of your suspects out that way?"

I shrugged. "Getting an alibi out of any of them was nearly impossible. Robert Owens claimed he was in North Carolina, but I can't prove that one way or the other. The rest of them were evasive when I asked them where they were."

Jenna said sternly, "Do you mean to say you've questioned each of these people directly about the murder? Have you lost your mind?" She immediately looked as though she'd regretted her outburst.

Butch nodded his head. "I've got to agree with the judge. You took a real chance doing that."

"What choice did I have?" I protested. "Nobody's going to do anything if I don't keep stirring things up."

"Then what about the front window? Couldn't you take that as a warning?" Butch asked.

Sandy said, "Wait a second, am I missing something?"

"Somebody threw a brick through her window," Butch said.

"That's horrid," Sandy said.

"It's fine now," I said.

David was silent as he studied the board. "Is this all you've got?"

"No, there's something else. Actually, two things. I found them last night when I was in Betty's house."

Everyone started asking questions with the exception of Jenna, who sat there expressionless. "I was there with a friend," I said, overriding their queries. "The place had been trashed. Somebody was looking for something, and I think it had something to do with Betty's murder."

They all listened intently as I described the scene I'd found. Finally, Butch said, "You know, I hate to bring this up, but it might have been because of the funeral and not because of the murder."

"That's what the sheriff said," I admitted.

Sandy asked, "What does that mean?"

I nodded to Butch, who explained. "There's a certain undesirable element that takes advantage of situations when someone who lives alone dies. They read the newspaper obituaries and make their strikes while the family's at the funeral home."

"That's terrible," David said.

Butch just shrugged. "It happens." Then he looked at me. "But you don't think this was random, do you?"

"No, I can't imagine it's not related to the murder."

"Then let me ask you this," Butch said. "Were there any valuables around? I'm talking jewelry, cash, anything a burglar might be interested in?"

I tried to think back on the scene, but for the life of me I couldn't say one way or the other. "I honestly don't remember."

He shook his head. "Carolyn, you've got to notice these kinds of things, especially if you're going to keep risking your life like this."

Jenna patted his arm. "Don't lecture her, Butch. She's had enough of that today."

He shrugged. "Sorry. You're a big girl; you can take care of yourself. So, you said you found two things. What were they?"

I pulled the key out of my purse, along with the slip of paper I'd found stuck to the bottom of my shoe. I'd put the paper in a plastic sandwich bag to be sure I didn't do any more damage to it than I already had. "This key was in one of her shoes, and this paper must have been some-where in the house."

Butch reached for the key. "It's from a locker like you'd find at a bus terminal. Do you mind if I hold on to this? I can ask around."

"I'd appreciate that," I said.

Sandy reached for the paper and studied it for a few seconds. "Now that's odd."

"What does it say?" David asked.

"Oh, sorry, I forgot to write that down too," I said. I wrote the letters I'd found on the sheet on the board, "is," "ight," and "one" indeed looked odd without any explana-tion.

Sandy was studying the sheet as I wrote. "It's a puzzle, isn't it? I'm good at those."

"So am I," Jenna said. "Carolyn, can you make copies of this for us? I'd like to study it more."

"That's a great idea," I said. "I never thought of that. David, would you mind?"

He took the paper and started for the office, where we had a small copier. "Be careful with it," I said.

"I'll handle it by the edges," he said. "After all, I don't want my fingerprints on it, too, do I?"

I suddenly realized that my prints were all over it. "I don't think it matters at this point. Hodges won't believe I found it at Betty's house, and even if I can convince him, I don't see how that can work out well for me. Maybe I should have given him the key and the paper last night."

Jenna wanted to say something; I could tell by the way she sat forward for a second before sitting resolutely back in her chair. I knew she didn't approve of my snooping, but she wouldn't say anything to the sheriff. At least I hoped she wouldn't.

"Here, copy this, too," Butch said as he tossed the key to David.

"That's a good idea. I'm afraid I destroyed the finger-prints on that as well."

Butch grinned. "Nothing to worry about there. It was a little tarnished, so I polished it with the edge of my shirt." Jenna was staring hard at him, so he added, "What? Old habits die hard."

"That's what I'm afraid of," Jenna said.

Butch scowled at her. "I told you, I'm reformed."

After David came back with copies for everyone and handed them out, I said, "That's it. I'm not sure where to go next, so that's why I called you all here."

"Now we look around a little, too," Butch said. "And you be careful."

"I will," I said.

"I mean it," Butch replied forcefully. "Don't take any more chances."

"You sound just like my husband."

"Then you should listen to both of us." He turned to David. "I need that key."

He looked at me first, and I nodded. After all, it wouldn't do me any good, and Butch might be able to find out what lock it fit into. David tossed it to Butch, and he caught it in one fluid motion.

"If you'll excuse me, I've really got to go," Butch said.

"We're finished here. Remember, let me know as soon as any of you come up with anything, okay?"

They all agreed, and as I let them out, David and I re-opened the shop for business. Although my investigation was basically no further along than it had been earlier that morning, I felt better having the Firing Squad helping me. If two heads were better than one, how much stronger were we now that all of us were working on the case?

• • •

Herman Meadows showed up at the shop just as I was getting ready to leave for lunch. "Do you have a second?"

"Just that. I'm on my way out."

He nodded. "Listen, I know things have been rough on you this past week, and all I wanted to say was that if you need a little more time for the rent, I can give you a week or two extra to pay it."

"I can write you a check right now," I said as I reached into the register for my checkbook.

"Carolyn, I wasn't dunning you for the money," Herman said.

"I know that, but look at it this way. You'll save me a stamp." I studied the balance of my business checkbook to make sure I could cover my rent and was relieved to see that I had a three-month cushion before things got really scary, though I hoped my situation would resolve itself long before then. I wrote the check, tore it off, and handed it to him. "There you go. It's even two days early."

"Are you sure about this?" he asked, holding the check up in the air.

"The business is doing perfectly fine," I said. What a lie. We were in sorry shape, but I wasn't about to admit it to my landlord.

"Good enough."

I'd given him his check, so why was he still standing in my shop? "Did you want to glaze a pot while you were here?" I asked.

"No, thanks. I don't have anybody to give it to," he said a little sadly.

"Don't worry," I said as I patted his arm. "You'll find someone special."

"What? No, I didn't mean it that way," he said, quickly recovering his roosterlike bravado. "What I should have said is that there are so many ladies in my life, I couldn't afford to make something for every last one of them."

"I'm sure that's true," I lied. If he wanted to live in that particular delusion, far be it from me to try to dissuade him.

He made a production of tucking the check into his shirt pocket, then said, "Thanks for this. See you next month."

If only that were true, but my landlord had a habit of popping in and out of the shop whenever he pleased. I wished he *could* find someone. Maybe then he'd leave me and the rest of his tenants alone.

I must have frowned at the thought of his frequent visits, because he quickly added, "Don't worry, I won't stay away that long. I love to visit. You know that."

"I wasn't worried at all." Hoping, wishing, praying, but not worrying.

"If that's it then, I'm late for an appointment," I said, glancing at my watch to add further emphasis to the ruse.

"Me, too. I'm always on the run. Never slow down, that's my motto. Where are you going? I'll walk you there."

There was no way I was going to let Herman Meadows escort me down the brook walk. "Thanks, but I've got to make a call first."

"Okay, then. See you."

David waited until Herman was gone, then he burst out laughing. "He's a real prize, isn't he?"

"Yes, it's a real shame I'm married, or I'd snap him right up. Maybe we could fix him up with your mother."

David grinned. "She'd kill us both." He peered out the window. "I think the coast is clear if you still want to go to lunch."

"You bet," I said.

I grabbed a sandwich at Shelly's Café and took it to a bench by the water. There was still a nice nip in the air, but the sun was shining warmly and the birds were serenading me as I watched the water flow past. It really was a lovely spot to be in, and I regretted that I sometimes took it for granted. Maple Ridge was all I'd really known, aside from four years away at college in Massachusetts, and I didn't plan on ever leaving Vermont again. I loved my small town, despite the disadvantages. Sometimes I envied my big-city friends their supersized stores and myriad dining choices, but most of the time I was quite content being a small fish in a little pond.

I was feeling quite mellow about my situation when I walked back into Fire at Will, despite the cloud of a murder investigation hanging over my head.

David met me at the door. "You had three calls while you were gone."

"I should leave more often then," I said as I took the notes from him. I glanced at them, then added, "These are all from members of the Firing Squad. Did any of them happen to tell you what they wanted?"

"No, they each asked me to have you call them back." He sounded a little hurt by their unwillingness to share with him.

"Don't worry, David, I'm sure it's not personal."

"Yeah, sure," he said. "If you don't need me, I'm going to lunch."

Like many artistic people I'd met, David was sometimes overly sensitive. It was a part of his nature, and I tried not to let it bother me.

I called Butch first, since, given his connections, he would probably have the best chance of shedding some new light on the murder.

Of course he wasn't in. I left a message, afraid that

we'd be playing telephone tag all day, then moved on to the next name on my list.

"Sandy, you called?"

"I did, but I'm swamped at the moment. Can I call you back in a bit?"

"Certainly," I said as she hung up on me.

Maybe I should stay at the shop all day so I could take my calls when they came in.

At least Jenna didn't let me down. "Hi, it's Carolyn. Do you have a minute?"

"I've got all the time you need."

"How nice," I said, meaning it sincerely. "I'm returning your call."

"So you are," she said. "Give me one second. I've got to put the telephone down."

So much for her rapt attention. I waited thirty seconds, humming the opening to the "Star-Spangled Banner" to myself, in lieu of anything better to do.

She came back on. "Sorry about that. My notes were in my office, and you caught me in the kitchen."

"I'm not interrupting your lunch, am I? I'd be glad to call back."

"No, I've eaten. I was just making out a grocery list. It's difficult to cook for one, do you realize that? I was startled to see that I've been making the same thing every day of the week for more years than I care to remember. Beef stew on Monday, pot pie on Tuesdays, leftovers on Wednesday, and on and on. It's a wonder my taste buds don't go on strike."

"I never thought about that," I said. For as long as I could remember, I'd always had someone in my life I enjoyed cooking for. Bill had always sported a hearty appetite, even when we'd been newlyweds and my skills were rather rudimentary and spotty at best. The boys had quickly devoured anything I put in front of them, and I'd had a tough time adjusting the portions back to something approaching normal after they left home.

"Nor should you have to," Jenna said. "I've been working with those sentence fragments you gave us, and I may have something."

"So soon?" I hadn't expected my gang to drop everything on my request.

"It's been fun, somewhat like working a new puzzle without fully knowing the rules. Here's what I have so far. 'It's as easy as th*is*. Make the first r*ight*, and my house is the next *one* you'll see.' They could be directions."

"I suppose that's a possibility," I said. "It seems to fit the message we found."

"But it's not very good, is it? How about this, then? 'Dear M*iss*, I'll see you ton*ight*. You're number *one*.' No, that's not much better, is it? I'll keep at it."

"Thanks, but you don't have to devote all of your free time to it."

"Carolyn, at the moment, that's all I seem to have is free time. I'll let you know if I come up with something more plausible."

"That sounds great."

Just as I hung up, the telephone rang in my hand. "You've been on the line," Sandy said.

"Guilty," I admitted. "I didn't know I was supposed to keep the phone free."

"You weren't. I just meant I've been getting busy signals. I tried your cell phone, too, but it said it was not in service."

"Hang on a second." I reached into my purse and saw that I'd failed to turn it on that morning, something I had a habit of doing now and then. "There, it's on now."

"Should I call you back on that number?" she asked.

"Now why on earth would you want to do that?"

"I don't know. I thought that's what you wanted me to do."

This could go on forever if I let it. "You called me, remember?"

"Of course I did. I've been playing with that puzzle piece you gave us, and I might have something."

Great, another sunrise was on my horizon, no doubt. "What have you got?"

"How about 'If you're looking for bl*iss*, come by my place to*night* and I'll show you why I'm the *one*.' That sounds kind of romantic, doesn't it?"

"Sandy, it could mean anything. I'm not sure we'll ever know what the note means."

"Don't give up, Carolyn. We have to keep trying. I'll see what I can come up with."

"Hang on a second, Sandy. David, what is it?" My assistant rushed back into the shop. He was holding something in his hand, but I couldn't make out what it was.

"Tell them you'll call them back. I've got something to show you."

"Sandy, I need to go."

"I'll talk to you later," she said.

"What's so urgent?" I asked David.

"I was snooping at Betty Wickline's house, and I'm pretty sure I found the other part of that note."

A part of me wanted to scold him for taking such a dangerous risk, but the part that was curious about the note's contents shouted down her counterpart. "Let me see it. You didn't break into the house, did you?"

"No, this was in the bushes outside. It must have been stuck to your shoe, too, only it came loose before you found the other part of it."

"Did anyone see you there?" Hannah would kill me if she knew what her son was up to, whether he'd done it on his own or not.

David looked smug as he explained. "I tucked my ponytail up in a hat and walked around the house with a clipboard in my hand. If anybody noticed me, they didn't say a thing."

I couldn't take the suspense anymore. "Here. Let me see it."

I studied the paper, and it certainly looked like a match to what I'd found. After retrieving my section, I slid the sheets together and saw that they were indeed a perfect match. The note, in its entirety, read, 'Betty, this *is* important. Meet me at mid*night*. We can't leave it like this. Come al*one*.'

As I grabbed the telephone, David asked, "Are you calling the police?"

"No, I'm letting Sandy and Jenna know they can stop working on this clue."

"But what does it mean?" he asked me.

"I might be wrong, but I think we just found the way the killer lured Betty to her death. If I'm right, it could explain why the house was trashed, too. Whoever wrote it didn't want the police to find it."

There was a sick look on David's face as he took that in. "Listen, maybe you should call Sheriff Hodges after all. This might be important."

"What do I tell him, David? That you were snooping around Betty Wickline's house and happened to stumble upon the second half of a note I removed from the dead woman's home? Or should I say that I found it myself and neglected to tell him about it until now? I'm sure he'll just love that, but I'm willing to do what I should.

That's the problem, though, isn't it? What exactly *is* the right thing to do?"

"I don't know."

"Neither do I," I admitted. "Let me call everyone else and see what they say."

Chapter 10

"You've got to tell the sheriff," Jenna said the second I told her about the completed note. "It's a legitimate clue now, and he has the right to see it."

"That's fine with me. I don't have a problem with doing that. Do you want to be the one to take it to him?" I asked.

"Hardly, but there has to be some way we can call his attention to it without implicating ourselves. How about mailing it anonymously?"

"We could do that," I admitted, "but I want to talk to everyone else first."

Jenna took a deep breath, then said, "Carolyn, this can't wait. It's important that the sheriff learn of this as soon as possible."

"Okay, I understand. Let me touch base with Butch and Sandy, and then we'll figure out a way to get it to Hodges."

"Do you promise?"

"I'll swear it under oath if it will make you feel better. Now I've got to call the others."

I hung up before she could start lecturing me, a tendency Jenna had that I wasn't all that fond of.

Sandy agreed with Jenna, but I still couldn't get in touch with Butch. What was that man up to? Did it have anything to do with our murder investigation, or was he doing something darker on his own? I made photocopies of the entire note for each of us, then selected an envelope from my supply, one without the Fire at Will logo and return address. I wasn't a complete amateur at this.

I had just addressed the envelope to the sheriff using big block letters that looked like a child's construction when Jenna walked into my office.

"You didn't have to come down here yourself," I said.

"I'm going to deliver that letter to the sheriff," she said sternly.

"Are you saying you don't trust me?"

Her grim expression melted. "That's not it at all. I'm volunteering to fall on my sword and turn it over in person. I'm willing to take full responsibility for it."

"There's no need for anything quite so dramatic," I said, warmed by her offered sacrifice. "I'm going to drop this off, but he won't know it came from me."

I showed her the printed envelope, and she nodded her approval. "Very nice. You've been spending entirely too much time with Butch, haven't you?"

"No, I get all my information from *Law and Order* and *CSI*."

Jenna rolled her eyes. "Give me the envelope. I'll slip it in his mail and he won't even know it."

"I don't want you to take any chances," I said.

"Believe me, I wasn't all that eager to take the heat for finding this. Your way is better. If it's totally anonymous, there won't be any way he can blame us for holding out on him. You did wipe it for fingerprints, didn't you?"

"Absolutely," I said smugly.

"And the envelope, too?"

Okay, maybe I hadn't covered all the bases. "No, not yet."

She continued. "You didn't lick the envelope seal, did you? That leaves DNA, not that Sheriff Hodges will necessarily check for it, but you never know."

I ripped open the envelope carefully and decided to begin again. Maybe being a bad guy took more attention to detail than I had thought. "Why don't we start over?"

"That's a capital idea," Jenna said as she pulled out a pair of latex gloves. "Why don't I do it? I thought these might come in handy."

"Be my guest," I said as I watched her meticulously repeat the tasks I'd done earlier. She was much better at them than I was, even sealing the envelope with a dampened paper towel. "Now who's been spending too much time with Butch?"

She blushed slightly. "I've had a great deal more exposure to the criminal element than Butch Hardcastle. There, that's perfect. I'll let you know how it goes."

"Should I go with you?" I was suddenly feeing guilty about letting Jenna take all the risk.

"No, you'd just stand out, and that is one thing we can't afford."

"Call me as soon as you're in the clear."

"I'm not robbing a bank, Carolyn. I'm just visiting some old colleagues. There's nothing to worry about."

"Of course there isn't."

An hour later I was frantically pacing around the shop as I waited to hear from Jenna. I was just about ready to call Hodges and confess myself when she walked in the door.

"Carolyn, what's wrong? Did something else happen?"

"That's what I want to know. You should have been back half an hour ago."

"Sorry, I got into a discussion with Gus Haggerty; he's the new district court judge."

"So you didn't get a chance to deliver the letter," I said, unhappy that the task would now fall back on me.

"Don't be ridiculous. I took care of it. More than likely, the sheriff's already read it by now."

"I highly doubt that," I said.

"Why's that?"

"Because he hasn't called or come by. I've got a feeling as soon as he opens it, I'm going to be the first person he wants to see."

As it turned out, I wasn't that far wrong.

Butch showed up a little later, and from the scowl on his face, I knew his news wasn't good.

"What's wrong?"

"It's about that key," he said, keeping his voice low.

"What about it? You don't have to whisper; no one's here." Business had picked up a little, but I was still going to have a hard time paying my bills out of my receipts, something I normally never had any trouble with. That meant I had to dip into my store's savings, something I hated to do.

"Sorry, old habits die hard," he said. "This isn't from a locker anywhere in Maple Ridge. I checked the bus depot, the Y, the high school gym, and no luck anywhere. I'm going to Burlington tomorrow for something else, and while I'm there, I'm going to poke around some and see if I can find out where it came from, and more important, what it's guarding."

"Just don't poke too hard."

"Carolyn, Betty hid this key in a place she thought no one would look. It kind of makes me think it's important."

"It could be," I agreed. "So, what are you going to be doing in Burlington?"

He ran a hand through his hair. "I'd really rather not say. Did the note get to the sheriff all right? I told Jenna I should have done it myself, but she wouldn't listen to me."

"You might draw some unwelcome attention if you walked through the sheriff's office," I said, trying to hide my smile at the thought of that.

"Yeah, that's what she said. I just hope she doesn't catch any grief about it."

"I won't let her," I said. "If it comes to that, I'll take full responsibility for having the note myself."

"I'll back you up," he said.

The front door chimed, and I wondered if I'd finally be getting another customer. It was the sheriff, and judging by the crease in his brow, I could tell he wasn't there to throw me a party.

Butch whispered, "You want me to stay?"

"No, I'm fine." Having him around might make things worse, and I had all I could handle without more conflict.

"I'll be outside if you need me," he said loud enough for the sheriff to hear. The men nodded abruptly to each other as they passed, and I watched Butch station himself in front of the shop. I wasn't exactly sure that his presence out there would be good for business, but it warmed my heart to have a friend standing close by.

"What's the story with this?" the sheriff asked as he held up the envelope Jenna and I had so carefully written.

"It looks like a letter," I said, trying to keep my gaze steady on his. "Did your mother write you?"

"You know full well what it is," he said. "What I want

to know is why you thought this crazy idea of yours would work."

That caught me completely off guard. "What are you talking about?"

"I'm talking about you fabricating evidence in a police investigation and then dragging an honored former judge in on your little scheme."

For one of the few times in my life, I was actually speechless. He continued. "So you're not even going to bother denying it?"

"Which part?" I asked without thinking.

"All of it," he snapped.

"I didn't make it up. I found it at Betty's house."

"Are you telling me you went back there after I told you expressly not to?"

"No, I discovered it when you threw me out." That didn't sound good for me, but I was past being able to cast a favorable light on my activities.

He asked me indignantly, "Why didn't you give it to me then?"

"I didn't find it until I walked outside. It was stuck to my shoe." There, I'd just admitted my part in how the letter had gotten to him.

"Now why don't I believe you?"

"I don't know. It must be a character flaw of yours not to trust people."

He stared at me coldly for a few seconds before he spoke. "You wrote this yourself, hoping to divert my suspicion to someone else. It's not going to work. You should know that. If anything, it makes you look more guilty in my eyes, not less. How did you talk Judge Blake into helping you?"

"She didn't," I said simply. "It was my idea, from start to finish."

That shocked him. "So you're actually admitting that it's a fake."

"I'm doing nothing of the sort," I said, not meaning to yell but doing it nonetheless. I caught Butch's eye through the window, and he looked as though he was ready to come in, but I shook my head. I was going to handle this on my own. "The letter is real. I knew if I just walked up to you and handed it to you, you wouldn't believe me."

"Guess what? You were right. I don't believe you."

"Then arrest me," I snapped. "Or, and here's an original thought, you could actually go out and find the real killer. I've got a list of suspects, if you're interested."

"With my name at the top of your list, no doubt," he said.

"You're on it," I admitted, feeling my voice soften.

"Who else?"

"Are you serious? You really want to know? I've got the names on a board in back."

I started toward the back room, and Hodges followed reluctantly. He studied the list, along with my rationales for each suspect, then shook his head. "You know what your problem here is? You have no proof. I told you to butt out of this, and I meant it."

"If you think I'm going to stand around and wait to be handcuffed, you've lost your mind. If you won't investigate this, I'm going to do it myself."

"Stay out of it, Carolyn. It's none of your business. I wouldn't want you to get hurt." There was a hint of steel in his voice, and something deeper. The man was actually threatening me.

I suddenly wished I'd asked Butch to stay. "I'm not afraid," I said. "Of anything."

"Well, you should be," the sheriff said.

He walked out of the shop, and Butch came in a few seconds later. "What was that all about?"

"Let's see, our dear sheriff just accused me of writing the letter myself, and then he threatened me."

"That does it. It's time I taught him a lesson."

Butch was heading for the door when I grabbed his arm. "Don't make it worse, okay? Please, for me?" The last thing I wanted was for Butch to get into a fight with Sheriff Hodges on my account.

"Are you sure?"

"I'm positive, but thanks for offering."

Butch took a step away from me, easily breaking my grip on his arm. "He should have believed you."

"Well, he didn't. I showed him my list of suspects, and he wasn't thrilled finding his own name among them."

Butch smiled gently. "I bet he wasn't. So what happens now?"

"Do you mean because of his threat? I'm not going to let that stop me. I can't make him believe me, but I can still try to find out the truth."

"Have you thought about who you're going to take it to once you do figure out who killed Betty? Can you trust Hodges to follow through?"

"That's a good point." I hadn't even thought about the possibility of the sheriff ignoring me, but the more I considered it, the more sense it made.

"Don't worry. I've got a friend with the state police we can go to." He must have caught something in my expression as he added, "Don't look so surprised. I have friends on both sides of the law."

"I'm starting to realize that," I said.

After Butch left, David came back. "Sorry I'm late. I got held up."

"Did they get much?" I asked.

"What are you talking about?"

I was feeling a little giddy after my confrontation with the sheriff. "You said you were held up. Were you scared?"

"Carolyn, I wasn't robbed. I meant I ran into a friend from high school, and we started talking about old times. That's why I'm late. Did I miss anything?"

I considered not mentioning what had just happened, but David would find out sooner or later. "The sheriff thinks I wrote the note to divert his suspicion toward someone else."

"It's not a bad thought, is it?"

"Only if I'd really killed her," I said, the jocularity gone from my voice. "Is that what you think?"

"No, of course not. I was trying to put myself in the sheriff's shoes."

"Well, don't," I said a little harsher than I should have. "I don't need anyone else believing I could have done such a terrible thing."

"I'm sorry," David said. The poor boy looked as though he was about to cry.

"It's all right," I said, stroking his arm lightly. "I know you believe in me."

"I do," he said earnestly, and for just a second, I could see Hannah's eyes in his. "Is there anything I can do to help?"

"I've got a few errands to run," I said. "Would you mind watching the shop by yourself again?"

He looked around the deserted place. "I think I can handle it. Should we have a sale or something to get folks to come back in? Maybe a sidewalk demonstration?"

"No, the situation's not that desperate yet." I hated flogging my wares on the sidewalk, and not because I didn't like being the center of attention. Well, not entirely because of that.

"So, where are you going?" he asked.

"I'm going to revisit my suspects and see if I can get any of them to admit to something they don't want to."

"How are you going to do that?" he asked.

"I don't know, but I'll be sure to let you know as soon as I figure it out."

Before I left the shop, I copied down the list on the blackboard in back. There was no need for motives on the list, though that would be crucial in determining the murderer's identity. All I needed was an idea of who I should talk to. The names "Sheriff Hodges, Evelyn Hodges, Larry Wickline, Robert Owens, Herman Meadows, Tamra Gentry, Connie Minsker, Kendra Williams" nearly filled up a page in my notebook. But who should I talk to first? That answer presented itself when Kendra called out to me from Hattie's Attic. It was time to find out if Kendra herself had had anything to do with Betty Wickline's death.

To Kendra's surprise, I walked over to her without her having to call me twice. Her shop, in stark contrast to mine, was brimming with customers.

"Shouldn't you be inside waiting on all of them?" I asked her. Shop owners who ignored their customers were one of my biggest pet peeves.

"Are you kidding? They love it when they have to track me down. Acting disinterested is one of my biggest selling tools."

That strategy would never work at Fire at Will. My browsers would just leave if I didn't wait on them hand and foot. At least that was my theory, and I didn't have the guts to try to disprove it.

"I need to talk to you," I said.

"Let me go first. You should know that Larry Wickline's

girlfriend was furious about the alimony he was paying Betty."

"I know. Connie told me about it herself." That seemed to take some of the wind from her sails.

"But did you know that Larry broke up with her right after the murder?"

"Actually, I knew that, too." She was really reeling now. It seemed that I'd out-gossiped the gossip queen. "She's mad enough to kill him, and if I were Larry, I'd watch my back. Those scissors look sharp."

"Do you honestly think she'd murder him?" Kendra looked absolutely delighted by the prospect.

"No, I don't think so, but then again, I've been wrong before. Kendra, how well did you know Betty?"

"We've already talked about that," she said abruptly.

"No, I'm pretty sure we haven't."

"I knew her; of course I did. Everyone in town knows everyone else. Maple Ridge is not that big a place, is it?"

She was acting oddly, even for her, and that was saying something.

"Did she ever shop here?"

Kendra's gaze avoided mine, and I knew I'd struck a chord, so I pushed harder. "Was she unhappy with something she bought from you?"

Kendra wanted to deny it—I could see it in her shifting gaze—but she couldn't bring herself to do it. "She was so rude. How was I supposed to know that piece was a fake? It came with a provenance. I offered her a refund."

"A full refund?" I'd heard rumors about Kendra's dealings with customers, and I wouldn't have bought a ten-dollar bill from her for $3.75.

"Not at first, but I finally gave her check back to her. She was so rude about it all."

"That must have just killed you," I said, choosing my

words carefully. "You've never given a full refund in your life."

"She insisted," Kendra said. For a large woman, she suddenly seemed very small. "I can't stand out here all day and talk to you. I've got to help my customers."

"I thought your sales tactic was to ignore them," I said with as much false sweetness as I could muster.

"Good-bye, Carolyn." She tore back into her shop and left me on the sidewalk, wondering if Kendra was hiding more than just a refund admission. She'd bear looking into, but it would have to be when I could catch her off guard again.

To my surprise, I found Larry Wickline at Hair Apparent, talking earnestly with Connie Minsker on a bench outside the beauty shop. It would be a great chance to speak with two of my suspects at the same time. From the look of things, they were delving deeply into their own problems, and while I normally hated to butt into other people's lives, it might give me an edge if they were both already off balance.

"Excuse me, do you two have a second?"

Connie dismissed me without looking up. "Sorry, we're in the middle of something."

"This won't take long. It's about Betty's murder."

That got their attention. They both looked at me suddenly, and Larry snapped, "Who are you?"

"We haven't met, but we did speak on the phone. I'm Carolyn Emerson. Betty was murdered in my shop."

"She's okay," Connie said, temporarily vouching for me. "What do you need, Carolyn?"

"The sheriff and I were going over a list of suspects earlier, and I wanted to clear something up." Okay, technically that was a bald lie, but he *had* glanced at my list; I'd seen him. Maybe we weren't exactly consulting on the investigation, but I did want information. Besides, how much more hot water could I get into with the man? He could only lock me up once for interfering with police business, couldn't he?

"He's a jerk," Larry said.

"I can probably get him off your back if you tell me where you were the night your wife was murdered."

"Ex-wife," they said in unison.

"Would you mind telling me where you both were?"

"You bet I'd mind. It's none of your business." Larry was a real charmer, and I wondered what Connie was doing with him.

She said, "Larry, don't be that way. She's just trying to help. Can't you see that? Carolyn, we were together in Boston. There's no way we could have killed her, either one of us."

Larry looked surprised by the admission. "Why did you just tell her that?"

"It's only right to tell the truth." The look of insistence in her eyes was hard to ignore.

"You shouldn't have said anything," he grumbled.

"Where exactly in Boston were you?" I asked. If I could get the name of their hotel, I might be able to confirm their alibi.

"I think it was the Independence Motor Inn," she said.

"No, it wasn't. It was the Liberty Bell or something like that."

Connie frowned. "No, that's not it, either. It had something to do with history and patriots and stuff like that. I remember that much."

Gee, that narrowed it down to about a thousand hotels and motels in the greater Boston area. "Do you happen to have a receipt from your stay?"

"No, we paid cash, and I'm pretty sure I tossed it when

I was cleaning out the car the other day," Larry said. "But we've both got alibis, so tell the sheriff to get off our backs."

I had barely left when the two of them started bickering about the name of the place they'd stayed. Larry had looked surprised when Connie mentioned the motel. Was it because he didn't think Connie should tell me they'd gone away the night his ex-wife had been murdered, or because they hadn't gone out of town at all? I didn't know, and worse yet, I had no way of checking out their story.

I hated to do it, but it was time to talk to Tamra again.

Her butler answered the door on the first ring. "Yes?"

"Hi, I'm Carolyn Emerson. Remember me? I was here before."

"Of course," he said as if he didn't believe me.

"May I speak with Tamra?"

"Wait one moment."

At least this time he let me wait in the foyer instead of outside. Her home was the most beautiful I'd ever been in, but then again, Tamra had more money than I would see in a thousand lifetimes. I wouldn't have traded with her, though, if it meant I couldn't have Bill or all of my friends. It suddenly struck me that Tamra was lonely. I could be accused of a great many things, but never that.

Tamra came breezing in with three scarves in her hand. "Which do you like, Carolyn? I'm packing light this trip."

"Where are you going?"

She frowned as she stared at her selections. "Back to the city. I never should have left. That's where all my true friends really are."

"Burlington?" I asked.

"New York," she answered almost disdainfully. "Oh, never mind. I'll take them all." She frowned at me and added, "Why are you here? It's not for more money, is it?

I'm afraid you caught me in a moment of weakness before."

"No, you were most generous the last time I was here."

"What is it, then?"

How on earth could I ask this woman for an alibi when
she'd donated so much money to the school library on my
behalf? "I was just wondering if you'd like to have lunch
sometime." It was the only thing I could think of. I really
needed to get more cover stories together.

Tamra looked touched by the offer. "What a delightful
thought. I'm sorry, though, I've got a car coming for me
any second. It's so much better than flying. I only arrived
here the day you visited me the first time, but I'm afraid I
miss the city too much."

"Have a nice trip," I said.

"It will be dreadful, but it's worth it. And Carolyn . . ."

"Yes?"

"Thank you for the invitation. I'll call you the second I
get back to town."

"That would be lovely."

I was outside walking toward my car when a limousine
pulled up. The driver, wearing a full chauffeur's ensemble,
got out and polished the door handle after he closed it.

"Excuse me, but do you always take Mrs. Gentry to
New York?"

He nodded. "I'm the only one she'll ride with."

"Do you happen to know when she came up? We were
discussing it earlier, and she wasn't sure."

He reached into his jacket and pulled out his log book.
After he gave me the date, he said, "I'd better go. I know
she won't be ready, but the lady expects me to be on time,
and she's paying for the privilege."

"Thanks. Have a nice drive."

He shrugged slightly, readjusted his cap, then walked to the front door.

Once I was back in the Intrigue, I took out my list and struck a line through Tamra's name. The driver had confirmed her alibi, and while I knew it was possible she could have paid for the murder instead of doing it herself, I was going to forget about her unless something more compelling came up.

That left three names on my master list of suspects I hadn't yet spoken with again, and of the group, only Herman Meadows would be without drama. Normally when I had a list of chores to do, I got the most unpleasant ones out of the way first, but talking to Evelyn Hodges and Robert Owens would be much worse than cleaning a bathroom. I'd find Herman, hopefully get an alibi so I could strike his name off my list, and then move on to Evelyn and Robert.

Wouldn't you know it, I got my landlord's voice mail when I called his office from my cell phone. I wasn't ready to tackle Evelyn, and I wasn't entirely sure I was going to talk to her at all. Tamra's place wasn't that far from Travers College, so I decided to swing by there and see if my pottery teacher had anything else to say for himself about Betty Wickline.

Chapter 11

"I'm looking for Robert Owens's office," I told the uniformed security guard in front of the student union. I'd thought about asking one of the students, but none of them would slow down long enough to answer my questions. There was something fresh and alive about the school, and I thought yet again about taking classes in my leisure hours. Not that I had that much time on my hands, but it would be fun to be on a campus again, not as somebody's mother as I had been a few years before, but as a student, there to learn. I could have easily asked Hannah for directions, but I didn't want her to know why I was there.

"Sure, that's easy enough," the man said. "Just go down Twilight Lane and look for the Markel Building. All the faculty offices are there."

"Thanks," I said. I hadn't realized that all of the staff had offices in the same quarters. I wasn't sure what I would tell Hannah about my visit if I happened to run into her, but I'd think of something. I could always ask her out to lunch in return for the last meal she'd bought us. Well, maybe I'd make it dinner. David might have to close the shop today at the rate I was going. I decided to call and check in with him before I went inside.

"Fire at Will," David said as he answered the phone.

"Hey, it's me. How's everything going?"

"We had a few customers come in," he said.

"Any sales?"

"No, they were just browsing. Don't worry, I know things will pick up," he said.

"Let's hope so. Listen, would you mind closing up this evening? I'm not going to be able to get back in time."

"Sure, it's no problem. My class isn't until later. That reminds me, you've got a message."

"Who from?" Had one of my queries finally paid off?

"Bill called. He's going to grab a sandwich so he can finish dressing. That doesn't make any sense, does it?" He hesitated a second, then added, "At least I think that's what it says."

David should have been in medical school, his handwriting was so bad. "Could it have been that he had to finish the dressers?"

David paused, then said, "If you say so."

"That has to be what it means. Is there anything else?"

"No," he said. "Herman Meadows came by. He said you called him, but he was tied up somewhere else. I told him to call you back, but he said he'd catch up with you later."

"Is that it?"

"That's it. Have you had any luck?"

"Maybe, but it's too soon to tell for sure," I said. "Is your mom teaching any of her classes today?"

"She should just be finishing up. Why, do you want to talk to her?"

"No, I was just curious." I'd been hoping Hannah would

be off campus, but no such luck. Maybe I'd be able to dodge her inside. I was afraid if she knew how actively I was pursuing the case, she might reacquire her fear that I would involve David. "Have a nice evening."

"I would, but I have class, remember?"

I glanced at my cell phone and saw that the battery was getting low. I'd have to charge it tonight, something I was constantly forgetting to do. It was amazing how easily I'd gotten used to the convenience of the thing, and how much I missed it when I didn't have it with me.

After taking a deep breath, I knocked on Robert's door, but instead of my potter, I found a sandy haired young man with the longest fingers I'd ever seen in my life. He had on overalls that were spattered with clay, a true potter's uniform, so I knew we were kindred spirits. "Hi, I'm looking for Robert Owens."

"You just missed him." He dismissed me without another thought, but I wasn't about to go away that easily.

"Do you know where I might find him?"

"Not a clue," he said.

Enough was enough. "I'm sorry, we haven't met. I'm Carolyn Emerson. Robert teaches some classes for me at my pottery studio." Okay, maybe calling Fire at Will a studio was a bit of a stretch, but it surely got his attention.

He looked up at me and smiled. "I'm Jack Hall. I've heard a lot about your place."

"All good, I hope."

"Absolutely. Listen, if you ever need anyone to teach some classes part-time, I'm a doctoral candidate in ceramics, and I'm always looking for ways to supplement my income."

"Why don't you give me your name and number and I'll keep you in mind," I said as I handed him a fresh sheet from my notebook.

"That would be great."

As he wrote, I said, "Maybe you can help me. I'm trying to find out if Robert was in town a few days ago."

"Well, we got back from North Carolina on Wednesday. Does that help?"

"Are you saying you went with him?"

He looked disgusted. "Yeah, he dragged me there to help him pack his equipment and some of his work. It was a little above and beyond the call of duty, if you ask me, but he didn't give me much choice."

"And you were there with him the entire time?"

"Every second. Why do you ask?"

"Oh, it's nothing. Do me a favor, don't mention this to Robert, would you?"

"Why not?" Jack definitely looked suspicious about my request.

"It's just that I'd asked him to teach for me Tuesday night, and I wasn't sure if he was in town and ducking me, or if he really did go away."

"He was gone. I can vouch for that."

"Thanks, I appreciate that."

"Hey, aren't you forgetting something?" he asked me.

"What's that?"

"My number," he said as he shoved the paper in my hand. "I'm serious about teaching, and I'm really good at it, if I say so myself."

"I'll keep you in mind, I promise," I said.

Just my luck, I bumped into Hannah out in the hallway.

"Carolyn, what are you doing here?"

"Would you believe I was looking for you?" I asked.

"No, not when you're coming out of Robert Owens's office. Is there anything wrong?" A dark cloud spread across her face. "Come here a second."

She pulled me down the hall and into her office. Once

the door was safely closed, Hannah asked, "This has to do with Betty Wickline's murder, doesn't it?"

"Yes. I have to keep digging. Every shred of evidence I turn up, the sheriff either discounts, ignores, or refuses to believe."

"You're not dragging my son into this, are you?" she asked sternly.

"David's watching the shop while I snoop around," I said. "I'm not forcing him to do anything you wouldn't approve of."

"It wouldn't take any force, and we both know it. I just don't want him involved."

"We talk, but he's not doing anything for me but working at Fire at Will." Though David had found the note on his own, I wasn't about to tell Hannah that. After all, I hadn't asked him to look around Betty's house; he'd done that of his own free will.

"So, what have you found out?"

"Do you really want to know, or are you just being polite?"

She grinned. "Have you ever known me to do anything just because I was trying to be polite?"

"You've got a point. Well, at least I've managed to cross a few names off my list. There are still entirely too many people I suspect, though."

"Just be careful," Hannah said.

"Don't worry, I get enough of that from Bill."

"Hey, your husband loves you. That's not a bad thing."

"I know. Well, I've got to run. I've got a few more names on my list to check out."

Hannah frowned. "Just don't ask David to work late. He's got a class tonight."

"Don't worry, we're closing early. He'll have plenty of time to get out here."

"That's what I like to hear. Can I walk you out?"

"That would be nice," I said.

We bumped into Robert Owens as he was going into his office. "Were you here to see me?" he asked harshly.

"I came to visit Hannah," I said. Now that I'd struck him off my list, I didn't want to antagonize him any more than was absolutely necessary.

He nodded and ducked inside. I just hoped Jack would keep his promise and not say anything about my visit. Then I realized he wouldn't, not if he wanted any shot at teaching future classes at Fire at Will.

"Herman, I need to ask you something." I'd finally gotten hold of my landlord at his office. It was a small, odd little building a few blocks away from the brook walk. The place was barely big enough to hold his desk and filing cabinets. A small sofa was made up into a bed, and I doubted even at his height Herman would be able to stretch out on it. "Are you living here now?"

He grinned. "I sold my house and haven't found anything I like yet. I made 200 percent profit on it in eight months. Can you believe that?"

"Why don't you at least rent a place until you find something else you like?" I couldn't imagine anything more depressing than living and working in such a confining place.

"I don't want to waste the money," he admitted. "This is fine. It's not like anybody ever comes here but me."

"It's not exactly a place you could bring a date back to after dinner and a movie though, is it?"

"I manage," he said. "Now what can I do for you?"

"I'm wondering where you were the night Betty was murdered."

He stared at me a few seconds, then asked, "Why do you want to know that? Carolyn, are you seriously getting mixed up in this?"

"All you have to do is tell me where you were so I can mark you off my list."

He hopped up from his chair. "You honestly think I could have killed her?"

It appeared that I was destined to anger everyone I knew, but if that was the price I had to pay to find the truth, so be it. "Take it easy. You had a key, so that automatically makes you a suspect."

He shook his head. "So does half of Maple Ridge, and that just matters if you actually locked your door, which I still doubt."

"Do you have an alibi or not?"

He shook his head. "No, ma'am, I was here going over my books. I didn't talk to anybody that I remember and nobody came by to visit." He gestured around the room. "This isn't exactly a great place to have company, you know?"

"Thanks anyway," I said.

"You're welcome. Now if you don't mind, I've got a ton of work to do tonight, so I'd better get to it. I'm going to heat up a can of beans for dinner. You want some?"

"No, thanks. I've got more work to do myself." I was sure there were worse things to do than split a can of beans with Herman Meadows, but at the moment, none came to mind.

I thought about going by the sheriff's house, but bracing Evelyn Hodges in her own den and demanding an alibi took a little more backbone than even I had. I could call her on the telephone, though.

"Do you have a phone book I could borrow?" I asked.

"Sure thing," he said as he slid a tattered old copy across his desk to me. "Who are you going to call?"

"I need the sheriff's number," I said as I found it, jotted it down on a piece of paper, then handed him the book. "Bye."

He grumbled a good-bye of his own and I left.

I walked back to the car, and instead of starting it up, I called the sheriff's house, hoping and praying Hodges himself didn't answer.

"Hello?" It was Evelyn.

"Hi, it's Carolyn Emerson."

"I've got nothing to say to you." There wasn't an ounce of warmth in her voice.

"I just called to apologize," I lied.

"Yes?" Did I hear a slight thaw in her voice, or was it my imagination?

"I didn't mean to imply anything earlier. Is there a chance we could get together and chat?"

"Who's that on the phone?" I heard the sheriff call out to her.

"It's a wrong number," Evelyn told him.

His voice was much closer as he said, "Then hang up."

We were disconnected, and I sat there staring at my phone a few seconds before I tucked it back into my purse. Herman was standing by the window, and he waved when we made eye contact. I nodded and drove off before he offered me a bean dinner again. I glanced at my watch and realized that David had closed the shop by now. I knew my husband was working hard to finish up the dresser set, but I wanted to talk to him, so I decided to take a chance and interrupt him while he was working.

"Hello? Bill, are you here?" I'd tapped at the back door of the furniture shop, then pounded on it before shouting my question. Bill had explained to me that his dusty old outbuilding in the back corner of our property was fine for construction, but that he needed the clean work area at the furniture shop to stain and hand wax the pieces after they were built.

His truck was in the back parking lot of the shop, but so far, he hadn't answered my summons.

"Hang on," he finally said.

I waited five minutes and was about to pound again when the back door opened. "Hey, Carolyn. What are you doing here?"

"Can't a woman visit her husband at work?" I asked.

"She can, but she usually has a reason," Bill said.

"I wanted to see you," I admitted.

He smiled that crooked grin of his, the one I'd first fallen in love with a thousand years ago. "Come on in. You can keep me company."

I followed him to the corner he had set up for finishing and saw a lovely matching pair of blond dressers in the elegant but simple Shaker style we both loved so much.

"Nice dovetails on the base," I said. Dovetails are a type of joinery that secures two pieces of wood at a ninety-degree angle. They get their name from the fanlike nature of the exposed joints, something I'd learned from Bill.

"They turned out pretty nice," he admitted. "I wouldn't mind keeping these," he added as he rubbed a palm over the top of one of them. "Just one more coat of wax and they'll be done."

"We could buy them ourselves," I said.

He laughed. "You want to know the truth? We couldn't afford them. So, what's on your mind?"

"What do you mean?"

"Carolyn Emerson, I've been married to you half my life. You don't think I can read you by now? You're here for more than a visit, not that I don't appreciate it."

"It's about Betty Wickline," I admitted. "Now before you start into another lecture, I'd better warn you, I'm not in the mood for it, do you hear me?"

"I understand what you're saying," he said. "What about Betty?"

"I've got so many suspects I don't know where to turn. I want to be able to talk to you about this, Bill. It's important for me to find out what happened to her."

He took it in, then nodded. "Go ahead, unload it." He picked up a can of wax and a soft rag, then worked as I listed my suspects and the motives I'd been able to come up with.

Finally, he said, "What does your gut tell you?"

"Honestly, I'm more confused than ever. Sheriff Hodges has been acting so strangely I'm inclined to think he had something to do with it."

"I kind of doubt it," Bill said, immediately contradicting me.

"Why is that?" I asked, trying to sound huffy. "Don't you think he's capable of murder?"

"That's not the reason why. It's just that the sheriff's too smart to leave the body in your shop like that if he did kill Betty. I've got a feeling he'd know where to dump a body so it would never be found."

"That's a pretty dark perspective," I said.

He shrugged as he applied the wax. "That's just my take on it. How about Evelyn? Would she kill Betty to protect her marriage?"

I thought about sweet and solid Evelyn, and then I remembered the vitriol she'd had in her eyes when we'd talked about Betty. "There's no doubt in my mind she could have done it. But how do I ask her for an alibi?"

"That's a tough one," he said. Bill was so calm when he worked, his normal gruffness barely there. "You could probably strike old Herman off your list. He thinks he's a lady-killer, but not the kind you mean."

"I'd tend to agree with you, but he didn't have an alibi when I asked him for one."

Bill snorted. "Carolyn, I doubt I'd have an alibi most nights, if it weren't for you. The man lives alone, remember?"

"In his office," I said.

Bill dropped his rag on the dresser top. "I knew Herman was cheap, but what happened to his house?"

"He sold it, so he's camping out in that odd little building where he has his office."

"I never said he wasn't strange. Speaking of unusual people, do you honestly believe Tamra Gentry could have killed Betty?"

"She was in New York at the time of the murder," I replied, "but that doesn't mean she couldn't have hired someone else to do it."

"And risk being blackmailed again? That was your motive for her, wasn't it?"

I admitted that it was. "Then how about Larry or his girlfriend Connie? Either one of them could have done it."

Bill shook his head. "But you said they were in Boston."

"So they say, but I never saw a receipt." My stomach grumbled loud enough for Bill to hear it.

"Haven't you eaten yet?"

"I was hoping you'd buy me something," I said.

"I'll give you a few bucks, but I ate an hour ago. I've got to finish these up."

"I don't want your money," I said. "I was hoping for your company. I'm starving. You promised me a night out on the town, remember?"

"Sorry, but this is the best I can do," he said. "How about a rain check?"

"Fine," I said. "Can you stop long enough to kiss your wife good-bye, or will that ruin your precious finish?"

"I think we can risk it," he said as he leaned down to kiss me good-bye. He smelled like peppermint and furniture wax, not a bad combination, surprisingly.

"See you tonight. And stay out of dark alleys."

"I will if you will," I said.

It was getting dark out when I left the shop, and I thought about driving home and making a sandwich, but I didn't want to eat by myself. I walked down to Shelly's Café and had a bowl of chili and half a club sandwich, and virtuously resisted dessert. Eleanor Klein was working behind the counter, giving Shelly one of her rare nights away from the place. I had a batch of iced cookies in the freezer at home, so if I got peckish later, I wouldn't have to go without a treat.

As I walked back toward where I'd parked the Intrigue, I had a feeling someone was watching me from the shadows again. "Bill, is that you?"

No reply. Maybe it was just my imagination running away with itself. I increased my speed, barely holding myself back from running. By the time I reached the Intrigue, my pulse was racing and I was a little out of breath.

A call was waiting for me on my machine when I got home, and I hit the play button as I headed to the kitchen for a cookie and a glass of milk. After all, running to my car had been some exercise, I justified to myself.

It was Butch. "Call me. I found the locker that matches that key you gave me."

He wasn't home when I called him back. How was I ever going to sleep not knowing what Butch had found? I kept calling Butch's number—without success—until Bill came home. That's when I realized that I'd just have to track Butch down the following day.

A customer was waiting for me the next morning at Fire at Will before I even had a chance to unlock the front door. He had a shopping bag with him, but it wasn't from my shop. I hated doing returns, especially with the weak sales we'd been having lately.

"I'll be open in twenty minutes," I said.

"This won't take long," he replied as he tried to come in when I unlocked the door.

"I'm sorry, but we're not open yet."

He frowned. "I don't appreciate your attitude. I'm going to speak with the owner about it."

"You just did," I said. I bolted the door behind me, and I could see him peering inside as I got ready for the day. I can't stand rudeness, and I won't tolerate it, even if it means losing a sale. I could have let him in a few minutes early, and if he'd been nicer to me I would have, but as it stood, I waited until the clock hit ten on the nose before I made a move to the door. He started pounding before I got there, so I dropped my keys, then made a production of finding them after I "accidentally" kicked them under one of the displays. It was three after, but I wasn't going to open up until he stopped pounding, which he finally did.

I flipped on the lights, turned the "Closed" sign to "Open," and finally unlatched the door. "Good morning," I said.

"It's about time," he said.

"How may I help you?"

He reached into his bag and pulled out a bisque fired piece that was white. My clays all fired pink, so I knew he hadn't bought it from me. As he waved it under my nose, he demanded, "What causes this?"

I looked at the bowl a second. "The walls shouldn't be so thick. I like to aim for a quarter of an inch myself."

"And that made it turn white?"

"No, that's what made it lopsided," I said.

"I didn't come here for a critique of my work. I want an explanation."

I knew the reason his bowl was white. He'd used a clay with almost no iron oxide in it. "Perhaps you should ask your supplier."

I should have told him just to get rid of him, but I wasn't about to reward the man's rude behavior.

He glared at me. "You know, don't you? What's it going to cost me to find out?"

"I don't care for what you're implying," I said.

"Fine, I'll play your game." He reached out and grabbed a flexible rubber kidney, a forming shape used to throw. It was an item that cost less than five dollars. "Now tell me."

It wasn't the lure of the puny sale that made me explain. I was tired of his attitude and wanted to get rid of him. "You used white stoneware clay for your pot. I don't carry it here, since I use red earthenware."

"So you're telling me I didn't do anything wrong?"

"Other than be rude to me? No."

"Fine," he said as he threw the rib back on the shelf. "I'm not buying that after all."

"The rib, or my explanation?" I asked.

He stared at me a few seconds. "Did you just lie to me?"

"Which time?"

He shook his head and stormed out. I was still laughing when David walked in. "What's so funny?"

"Nothing. Well, it was something, but I couldn't begin to explain it if I had to. Are you ready to get to work?"

"Such as it is," he said.

"We're going to have a good old-fashioned spring cleaning," I said. "The place needs a thorough sweeping and dusting, and this is the perfect time to do it."

"If you say so," David said. "I'm not a big fan of cleaning, myself."

"I know that, but think of it this way. You'll be getting paid to clean the store. That's better than tidying up your room at home for free, isn't it?"

He grinned. "You've got a point. Where should I start? Do you want me to grab a broom?"

"First we dust, then we sweep," I said. I handed him a rag and grabbed one for myself, too. "I need to make one telephone call, and then I'll join you. Why don't you start at the top shelves and work your way down?"

I dialed Butch's number, fully expecting to get his answering machine again, when he surprised me by picking up. "Yeah?"

"It's Carolyn. I tried to call you back last night, but I couldn't get you."

"I just got back in," he said, adding a yawn to prove it.

"What were you doing out all night long?" I asked without thinking.

"Gee, Mom, I'm sorry. I forgot all about my curfew. That's cute, Carolyn. I like that."

"Okay, it's none of my business. I just wanted to know what you found in the locker."

"It was empty," Butch said. "Somebody cleaned it out before I got there."

I'd been counting on there being something in the locker that pointed to Betty's murderer. It was asking too much, I guess. "There wasn't anything at all?"

"Nope," he said. "I don't mean to be rude, but I've got to get some sleep. I'm dead on my feet."

"I'll let you go then. Thanks."

"No problem."

After he hung up, I wondered if Butch was telling me the entire truth. If the locker was empty, why had Betty kept the key and hidden it so well among her vast collection of shoes? Was it possible Butch had taken advantage of his situation and helped himself to the contents of the locker? I hated to think such a thing of one of my friends, but old habits died hard, and I couldn't be sure he'd completely reformed. Still, if there had been anything in the locker, he would have told me.

Wouldn't he?

Chapter 12

I heard the front door chime a few minutes later and saw Annie Gregg walk in. David was up on a ladder cleaning a top shelf, and when he saw her, he nearly fell off his high perch.

"Hi," he said louder than he needed to. "May I help you?"

"I've got it," I told him, though I doubted he'd heard me. We had a ton of pretty girls come in and out of Fire at Will, but I'd honestly never seen David act like this before. I stared at Annie, who was clearly embarrassed by all the attention, and tried to see what David saw. Then it hit me. Annie had reminded me of someone the moment I'd met her, and now I realized who: she bore a striking resemblance to a young Julia Roberts, David's hopeless crush.

"What brings you here?" I asked.

She glanced up at David, who was doing everything but drooling. I doubted any man had ever stared at me like that, not even Bill back in our courting days.

"Could we talk in your office?"

"Sure thing." I turned to David. "We'll be right back."

When we walked in back, Annie asked, "Is he like that with every girl who walks in here?"

"It's never happened before. To be honest with you, I think he's smitten. You could do a lot worse, you know."

She shrugged. "I'm not looking for a boyfriend. I need to talk to you about Betty Wickline."

"What is it? Did you remember something?" It was all I could do not to shout.

"It's probably nothing, but you said I should call or come by if I remembered anything."

"That's right, and I appreciate you coming."

She hesitated, and I wanted to grab her shoulders and shake it out of her. "Annie, you can trust me. I know you don't know me, but ask around. I'm one of the good guys."

"I know. I spoke with a few people around town. I hope you don't mind." She looked positively embarrassed by the admission.

"As long as nobody trashed me, why should I mind?"

"Oh, no, I heard a lot of good things about you, Carolyn. That's why I'm here."

I tried to bite back a huff of frustration. "I'm listening."

"On second thought, I should probably go," she said as she started to leave.

"That's your decision," I said. "I won't pressure you if you don't want to tell me."

Was she going to dangle something in front of me, then jerk it back? I knew pushing was exactly the wrong way to handle Annie. If she wouldn't tell me now, I could only hope that she'd change her mind and say something later.

"You're really not going to press me about it?" she asked.

"I wouldn't dream of it," I said, which was the biggest

lie I'd told so far that day. If I thought it would do any good, I'd iron and fold her after I finished the press.

To my surprise, she sat down in my chair. "That's all I needed to know. I want to ask you one favor before I tell you this."

At that point, I would have offered her just about anything, including my firstborn, though he was a little long in the tooth for her. "Ask away."

"Don't tell anyone where you heard this. I'd be too mortified if word got out, and I might lose work if folks thought I was sharing secrets."

"I won't say a word," I said.

"Okay. Well, this might all be a fuss about nothing, but I heard Betty say something the last time I was cleaning her house. She was on the telephone, and to be honest with you, she was so mad at whoever she was talking to, I think she forgot I was even there."

"Did you happen to hear what she said?"

Annie nodded, and I wondered if I was going to have to bribe her to get it out of her.

Finally, she said, "Betty was arguing with Kendra Williams."

That was a disappointment. "I already know about that. Betty bought a fake off Kendra, and they'd been squabbling about it ever since."

"Are you sure?" Annie asked. "I thought it was more than that. And here I've impugned that poor woman's name. That's why I hate rumors and gossip."

I couldn't imagine anyone ever calling Kendra a "poor woman," unless it related to her taste in clothes. Or makeup. Or attitude. But that didn't make her a murderer.

"Sorry I couldn't be more help," she said.

"I appreciate you coming by, Annie."

I led her out of my office and was surprised to see that

David had given up all pretense of dusting. "Excuse me, but is there any chance you'd like to go out with me?"

"I'm sorry, thanks for the offer, but I can't. I'm really busy working so I can pay my way through college, and I'm afraid that doesn't leave any time for dating."

The David I knew would have slunk into the corner to lick his wounds, but an amazing transformation occurred before my eyes. "It doesn't have to be dinner and a movie. How about a cup of coffee? If you're not busy, we could go right now."

Annie looked over at me, and I said, "It's up to you, but he's a nice guy. As far as I know he's had all of his shots, and his mother raised him to treat women with respect, but it's your decision. I don't want to get involved."

"So, would you?" David asked again.

"Why not?" Annie finally agreed. I don't know who was more surprised by the acceptance, David or Annie.

He looked at me. "Is it okay with you?"

"I already gave my blessing, not that it should matter."

"I meant is all right if I leave now."

I laughed. "I can handle the dusting. Have fun."

"We will." David was indeed smitten. That was clear by the way he looked at Annie as he opened the door for her. It was about time he focused his attention on someone a little more attainable than a famous married actress he could never be with. The initial attraction was obviously there, and if I knew David, it wouldn't take him long to realize how special Annie appeared to be on the inside.

I wasn't in the mood to do any spring cleaning after David and Annie left. At the rate my sales were going, I would be collecting a lot more dust anyway, so why bother? I went back to the chalkboard and studied my list again. With a piece of chalk, I marked a single line through the names Robert Owens, Tamra Gentry, Larry Wickline, and Connie Minsker. It didn't mean they were all absolved of the murder, but it did mean that if any of them had done it, I had no way to prove it. Even Connie and Larry's flimsy alibi was enough to stifle me. The fact that they couldn't agree about the name of the motel they'd stayed in encouraged me to believe they were innocent. If they'd arranged their alibis beforehand, surely they would have come up with a name or better yet, not mentioned where they'd stayed at all. That left the sheriff and his wife as my prime suspects, with Kendra and Herman thrown into the mix because of their keys, not because of anything they'd done to arouse my suspicions. But how was I going to interrogate my two prime suspects without getting thrown in jail myself? Should I talk to Butch's friend with the state police and let him take over? What evidence did I have to give him, though? It was all based on hearsay and suppositions that I wasn't entirely sure were accurate. No, I couldn't go to anyone in authority unless I had more than I did at the moment.

Sheriff Hodges was a lost cause for me, but I still might be able to get something out of Evelyn. Maybe if I ambushed her again, I'd catch her off guard. It wasn't the best idea I'd ever had, but it was just about the only one I had left.

I hated to lock up Fire at Will during my regular business hours, but with David gone, I really didn't have much choice. Honestly, I suspected I probably wouldn't miss out on a single customer, but it still went against the grain to shut down.

After locking the front doors, I called Evelyn's house on my cell phone, since I had the number stored there from the night before, but there was no answer. Either she was screening her calls, or she really was out. Knowing Evelyn, I tried to guess where she might be. She could be volunteering somewhere, she could be at the beauty shop, or she could be shopping at the grocery store or somewhere along the brook walk. I decided to stroll down to the grocery from Fire at Will. All I needed was a light jacket, though I knew the weather in April could change on a dime and I might be back in my heavy coat tomorrow. Kendra didn't come out as I passed by her shop. Either she was waiting on a customer, or she was avoiding me. Wouldn't that be lovely if the woman started ducking me? It was almost worth having her think of me as a murder suspect.

There was no sign of Evelyn on the walk, and since I was at the grocery store anyway, I decided to pick up a few things for the house. I grabbed a basket, threw a few items in as I scouted out the aisles, then reluctantly headed for the cash register to pay. Now I'd have to lug my bag of groceries back to the Intrigue, which was parked on the far end of the walk.

I was halfway back to the shop when I spotted Evelyn looking in the window at Rose Colored Glasses. Trying not to alarm her, I walked softly up beside her and joined her as she gazed at a lovely stained-glass cardinal. "Hello, Evelyn."

She nearly dropped her purse. "Carolyn, what are you doing here? Are you stalking me?"

"Of course I am," I said, using one of my favorite techniques: telling the absolute truth in such a way that no one believed me. "I hunted for you at the grocery store, but you weren't there, so I bought a few things along the way. I was so excited when I finally found you that I nearly dropped my bag."

"There's no need to be sarcastic," she said. "I've been a little on edge lately."

"There's been a lot of that going around," I admitted.

"Actually, I'm glad we ran into each other," Evelyn

said. "I wanted to talk to you last night, but my husband was standing right there."

I wanted to ask her if she was going to confess and save us all a lot of trouble, but for once I listened to my inner voice, which was shouting at me to shut up and hear what the woman had to say.

"Shall we sit?" I suggested as I pointed to one of the benches that faced the brook walk.

"Yes, that would be nice."

I put my groceries down between my feet as I sat. "Now, what did you want to talk about?"

"I realized too late that you got the wrong impression when we were in front of your shop the other day. I was out of line when I spoke about Betty."

"You obviously meant it," I said simply, preferring to let her explain further.

"I was being silly. I realize that now. I love my husband, and more importantly, he loves me. We'd just had a fight right before I spoke to you, and I was still fuming, just mad at the world. Under ordinary circumstances, I never would have said that about poor Betty."

So it was poor Betty now, was it? Talk about your revisionist history. "What did you have against her?"

"To be honest with you, the woman drove me mad. Surely she irritated you, too. You know as well as I do how she could be, always sniping, nothing ever good enough for her."

She had me there, and I could only agree. "Betty could be a pain, but I didn't want to see her dead."

"I didn't, either," Evelyn replied.

"But you had more cause to wish her ill than her attitude and behavior."

Evelyn kept her gaze on the brook. "She wasn't having an affair with my husband. Give him some credit. The man has more taste than that. We don't have a perfect marriage; who does, including you? But if nothing else, I know his taste in women by the ones he notices, and he likes skinny little blondes, something we both know I'm not, and neither was Betty."

"It's not really proof though, is it?" I asked softly.

"It's enough for me," she said. "We're getting off course here. I wanted to apologize for my behavior, and now I have."

She left, but I stayed in place on the bench. Blast it all, Evelyn made a good point. I knew the type of women Bill preferred, too. It wasn't an insult to me—he didn't exactly chase them down the street—but I would have to be blind not to notice. The problem was, if I believed her, the only suspects on my list were Kendra and Herman, and if I thought about it long enough, I was sure I'd be able to find reasons to strike them off as well. Somebody had killed Betty. I couldn't see her jamming that awl into her heart in my store just to make me squirm. If she had, it would be one of the oddest ways to commit suicide I'd ever heard of.

So where did that leave me? Since only two people were left on my list, I decided to talk to them both, just in case I'd dismissed them too easily.

Oddly, when I walked to Kendra's shop, I saw that Hattie's Attic was closed as well, though by all rights she should have been open. That was extremely unusual for her. Where could she be? Maybe Herman would know. I walked to his office, but he was gone, too. Was nobody where they should be? I felt thwarted. What now? There was really nothing left I could do but go back to Fire at Will. Maybe I could figure something out back at my shop, and maybe, if I was lucky, a customer might come in and actually buy something. Hey, stranger things had happened.

• • •

I wasn't looking forward to the scolding David was going to give me, but I braced myself for it as I carried my groceries back to the shop. To my surprise, David wasn't back yet from his coffee date. Surely that was a good sign. I liked Annie, and I thought of David as one of my own, so it would tickle me to death to see them get together. I wasn't sure how Hannah would feel about it, though. She wanted great things for her son, and I was afraid her standards were nearly impossible to meet. I'd have to have a talk with her about that if things got serious.

I stowed my groceries in the back, then put on a Fire at Will apron, just to look the part of a store owner while I still could. Okay, things weren't *that* dire, but I needed this murder solved so I could get back to business as usual.

David showed up twenty minutes later. "Sorry, I didn't mean to stay so long. We started talking, and the next thing I knew, two hours had gone by."

"So I'm guessing you two hit it off," I said.

"We're going out again tonight," he said. "Don't worry, it's after class. She's amazing."

"And not just because she looks like Julia Roberts?"

David laughed. "You caught that, too, did you? I guess there's a slight resemblance, but if you want to know the truth, Annie's a lot prettier."

"I'm sure Julia will be crushed to hear the news."

"I'm sure," David agreed. "Now let's start cleaning this place up. We need to be ready for the wave of customers we'll be having soon."

"Do you know something I don't?" I asked as I grabbed a rag.

"No, but things are bound to turn around. I can feel it." He was positively giddy.

"My, you are in a good mood."

"I can't help myself," he said. As David climbed the ladder, the front door chimed.

"Excuse me," said a nice-looking young woman in a business suit. "I was wondering about those wind ornaments in the window. They must be terribly expensive."

"Five dollars apiece," I said.

"You're kidding me. I'll take a dozen."

"Would you like to learn how to make them? I could teach you in twenty minutes."

She looked perplexed by the offer. "I don't understand. They are for sale, aren't they?"

"Absolutely. I just thought you might like to see how it's done."

She paused in thought for a few seconds, then asked, "Could you show me, instead of me doing it myself?"

"I'd be delighted. I'm Carolyn, by the way," I said as I offered her my hand.

"I'm Jessica," she said.

"Have a seat, and I'll get us set up."

I grabbed a few of the bisque fired blanks I kept on hand, cut out in a variety of cookie cutter shapes. They each had a hole punched out near one edge to make them easy to hang. "Oh, do you buy them in bulk?" she asked.

"No, I make them right here myself." I reached over and grabbed a cutter in the shape of a leaf, then took a little clay from a bag by the wheel. "I'll do one for you, but we won't be able to fire it today."

"I don't mind," she said. "I'd just like to see the process."

I took the clay, kneaded it a little, then rolled it out with my French rolling pin, a tapered piece of maple I preferred instead of the dowels I had my students use. "After it's a quarter inch thick, you just cut out the shapes you want." It was as easy to do as it was to explain, and in a few seconds I had a leaf cut from the clay.

"But there aren't any veins on yours."

"I can fix that," I said as I quickly embedded the lines into the leaf with a rib to make it look more realistic. After that, I used a punch for the hole. "Now it's ready to fire."

"Let's add some color to it," she said.

"We can, but it has to be fired first. When you do that, you get something like this." I plucked a leaf out of the fired selection and handed it to her. She studied it as she held it. "It's light, isn't it?"

"All the moisture's been baked out of it. Sit down. You can decorate it yourself."

"Show me how," she said.

I chose a diamond pattern for myself, then grabbed a squeeze bottle of glaze. After putting some emerald green in a pie tin, I took a brush and began applying it to the diamond.

"That's all you do?"

"That's it. You can get a lot fancier if you'd like, but after this is fired, it will be ready to hang."

She put some yellow, orange, and burgundy on her plate and carefully colored her leaf. "I want it to look like autumn."

I took her leaf and put it on another pie tin and wrote "Jessica" on it with a Sharpie. "Come back in a couple of days and it will be ready for you."

"That's excellent. What do I owe you?"

"The first one's on the house," I said, surprising David with my generosity. "It's a special deal today until closing." I figured we had about twenty minutes left. How bad could it be?

"That's excellent. I'm shopping with some friends. Let me get them."

She hurried out of the shop, and I started to regret my rash offer. David must have sensed it, too. "What's the worst that can happen? We'll get some new customers for the shop."

"That's true, but don't you ever do that."

"No danger of that," he said, still grinning. "It's your business."

Two minutes later, eight expensively dressed women came in with Jessica. They all seemed excited about the prospect of painting some pottery, and David climbed down to help. We used nearly all of the bisque-fired ornaments I'd made, but I had so little in the clay and I bought my glazes in bulk, so my generosity wouldn't cost us that much.

After they decorated leaves, boxes, circles, and all four of the card suits, the women tore through the store buying nearly everything in sight. Once they were gone, David locked the door and whistled loudly. "Wow."

"I second that," I said. In one single burst of sales, I'd made up for the money I'd lost since the murder.

"If that was your plan, you're a genius."

"I wish I could take credit for it, but it was sheer dumb luck on my part." I still couldn't get over what had just happened. "Tell you what, why don't you go on and get ready for your date? I can handle things here."

"Are you sure?"

"Absolutely. Have fun. After class, that is."

"Yes, ma'am, I will."

After he was gone, I dead-bolted the door behind him and turned on some background music. It always made the work go faster, and when I was alone, I could play whatever I liked, which at the moment was a selection of Billy Joel, the early years.

I heard a tap on the door, and I saw my husband standing there with a bag in his hands.

As I opened up, he said, "Nice dance moves you've got going on there."

"I wasn't dancing," I said sternly. Well, maybe I had been. It was a small blessing he hadn't caught me singing.

"Billy Joel never had a prettier backup singer, either," he said.

"Don't push your luck."

"Hey, I can tease you a little. After all, I brought food."

It smelled delicious, and I was starving. Had I forgotten lunch? It was unusual for me to miss a meal, whether by accident or design.

"Okay, but that's enough out of you. What did you bring me?"

"I've got a salad for you, and two burgers for me. Unless you want one of the burgers."

"I'd love one. I'll share the salad with you, if you'd like some."

"Thanks, but I'll pass. Knock yourself out, though."

As I set the table in back with paper plates and napkins, I asked, "What's the occasion?"

"I've got to work again tonight. Those pieces still aren't finished."

"I thought you were done." The two dressers were beautiful. What else could he do to them?

"They wanted three more coats of wax when they saw them today. I argued about it, but I lost. Sometimes I wonder why I'm even doing this. I'm supposed to be retired."

"Then tell them no," I said after I chewed a bite of burger. "We don't need the extra income."

"Did I miss something, or did your business just get better?"

I told him about Jessica and her friends' buying frenzy, but his smile didn't even come close to matching mine.

"Don't get too excited," he said.

"And why shouldn't I?" What was wrong with this man? Why couldn't he share my good mood with me, instead of bringing me down?

"This was a temporary fix. You can't count on something like that to bail you out every time."

"Well, it did this time, and that's all that matters," I said. "Now eat your food before it gets cold." I knew he was right, but did he have to point it out like that?

After we were finished eating, Bill said, "I guess I just needed one burger after all."

I reached over and patted his stomach. "Would it have killed you to try my salad?"

"Who knows, it might have, so why take the chance?" He looked at the empty plates. "Sorry, I forgot all about dessert."

"How does a brownie sound?" I asked. I'd picked one up at the store, a massive, heavenly concoction I'd not yet been able to duplicate in my own kitchen.

"Don't tease me, woman," he said.

I reached back to my grocery bag and retrieved the brownie. "Sorry, I don't have any milk to offer you." My husband, among his many idiosyncrasies, loved his milk so cold it had to be nearly frozen before he'd drink it.

"I can live with that," he said. I broke the brownie in half, and to my credit, I gave my husband the larger piece. If he noticed my generosity, he didn't comment.

With dinner and dessert finished, he said, "Tomorrow night I'll take you out to a real dinner and you can cash that rain check I've been promising you."

"I don't know, this was nice," I said. Really, all I needed

for a fun night out was my husband and some good food, and I'd just had both.

"Yeah, but we'll do something fancy."

I looked at my husband and saw his steady grin. "Is there something you're not telling me? Did we win the lottery, by any chance?"

"No, nothing like that, but I got the commission on four more pieces today, and they paid me a bonus for getting the dressers done so quickly. I figure I can afford to take you out on the town."

"I won't even complain about how expensive it's going to be," I said.

"Are you going to be all right here by yourself?" Bill asked me.

"I'll be fine. I'm just about finished, and then I'll go home and watch one of my movies that you hate."

"Sounds like a plan to me." I led him to the door, bussed him with a quick kiss, then locked the door behind him.

He tapped on the glass. "Is it dead-bolted?"

"Yes, it's dead-bolted."

He grinned, winked at me, then started back to the furniture shop. Sometimes my husband could be so sweet, something that was hard to remember when he was being a grumpy old bear.

I finished cleaning the tables and rinsing the brushes, and everything was ready for tomorrow. I was just about to leave when the telephone rang. I half expected it to be Bill, so I was surprised to hear someone else's voice on the line.

"Hey, Carolyn, I'm glad I caught you."

"I was just getting ready to leave, Hannah. What's up?"

She hesitated, then said, "Have you heard about David's new girlfriend?"

"I wouldn't say they're dating. They just had coffee this afternoon."

"You knew about it?"

I found a chair. This might be a long conversation. "He met Annie when she came by the shop to see me."

"So, she does have a name," Hannah said. "My dear son wouldn't tell me anything about her."

"She seems like a perfectly lovely girl," I said.

"David mentioned that. He said she looks like Julia Roberts, only prettier. That can't be good."

"Don't worry, Hannah, he's nearly a grown man."

She paused, then asked, "So, are you trying to tell me that you don't worry about your sons anymore?"

"Of course I do," I admitted. "But it doesn't do the least bit of good."

"I guess you're right. I don't suppose there's any way you're free this evening, is there? You and Bill probably have plans."

"As a matter of fact, he's working late on a pair of dressers at the shop. We had hamburgers, but if you'd like to meet for coffee, I'm free."

"That would be great. In the Grounds, say in half an hour?"

"Sounds good. I'll see you then."

I could piddle around the shop for twenty minutes, but that didn't really sound like much fun to me. If I stayed, I'd end up dusting or paying bills, and for once, I was done working for the day. As much as I loved having my own shop, it was a demanding job. I decided to take my time walking along the brook, maybe even do a little window shopping along the way.

After I locked up, I peeked inside a few windows as I walked to the coffee shop. The evening had turned chilly as I'd predicted, and I was glad I'd worn my heavy coat. I slid my hands into my pockets and found a bisque-fired di-amond shape I'd been playing with when Jessica and her companions were in the shop. I must have slipped it into my pocket without even realizing it while the ladies were going through my stock. The edges were sharper than I liked, so I'd pulled it from their selections. As I walked, I fiddled with the piece, keeping my hands in my pockets.

I was amazed that some of the shops along the brook managed to stay in business. Did Rose really sell enough stained glass to keep above water? The one tenant I didn't have to worry about was Kendra Williams. She seemed to always have a steady flow of customers at Hattie's Attic. I spotted a pair of candelabra displayed in the front window, and wondered how they would look on my dining room table. As I peered farther into the gloom of the antique shop, I saw something out of place. It was a pot Betty Wickline had thrown at Fire at Will the month before. How odd that Kendra would have it for sale in her antique shop.

Could there be a tie between them that I might have missed before? It was time for a closer look.

Chapter 13

"Kendra, are you there?" I banged on the front door, but heard no answer. She'd probably gone home already. I glanced at my watch and saw that I still had fifteen minutes before I had to meet Hannah, so I walked the block to Kendra's home to ask her about that pot. It would be just like her to try to pass it off as some kind of antique, but I wasn't going to let her get away with it.

I was surprised when I saw Herman coming out of Kendra's place as I approached. "Carolyn, did you bring her some soup, too?"

"What are you talking about?"

"Haven't you heard? Kendra's under the weather. I'm sure she'd love to see you, though. I'll walk back in with you."

A sick Kendra was more than I could take. "You know what? I forgot the soup. I'll come back later."

"Was there something you wanted her for? I might be able to help."

"I saw one of Betty's pots in the window at her shop, and I wanted to ask her how she got it."

Herman laughed. "I can clear that one up for you. Betty made her display it as a penance after she got her refund. I'm surprised Kendra didn't throw it out after what happened."

"No doubt she will as soon as she remembers it's there," I said.

"Why don't you go on in? I know she'd love your company," Herman said.

"Oh, I'll be back," I said. "I'm meeting someone now. I'll make it later, though."

I left him there and headed to the coffee shop. If Kendra was under the weather, she wouldn't be in the mood to talk about Betty. I believed Herman's explanation about the pot—it sounded just like something Betty Wickline would do—but was it possible there was more to it than that? Should I press her about it when I knew she was feeling ill? Then again, maybe she'd be lonely, and a little vulnerable. I felt bad about taking advantage of her, but it might be the only way I'd get to the truth. I probably did have time to talk to her before I met up with Hannah, but I didn't want Herman Meadows leaning over my shoulder when I grilled her. Kendra might be more inclined to talk if it were just the two of us.

Hannah was already at In the Grounds when I got there. "Hey, thanks for meeting me," she said.

"I'm happy to have the company, since Bill's been abandoning me lately."

"I already ordered for you," she said. "Have a seat. And don't worry about your husband. He adores you."

"I'm not disputing that," I said. "I just wish he showed it a little more."

"He is who he is."

"Wow, let me write that down. You English professors are so profound."

Hannah threw her napkin at me. "Okay, I get it." After she took a sip of coffee, she asked, "So, how well do you know this Annie? What does she do?"

Hannah was going to go ballistic when she found out Annie was a maid. "She's saving for college. The girl must be smart; she was accepted at Stanford."

"So why isn't she there right now? Is it the money? They have student loans and such."

"She wants to pay her own way."

Hannah bit her lip. "How is she going to afford it on her own? What does she do?" She frowned, then added, "Don't tell me, she's an exotic dancer."

"No, she cleans houses," I said simply.

"She's a maid? That's even worse."

"Really? Would you mind explaining that to me, because I don't see it. Not that I have anything against either occupation, but I find your stand interesting."

"Don't be difficult. You know what I mean."

I wasn't about to let her off the hook that easily. "Actually, I don't. She's working hard at an honest profession making people's lives a little easier, and earning more than I do while she's at it, by the way. What's the problem?"

When Hannah didn't answer, I lowered my voice and said, "I couldn't love you more if you were my sister, but sometimes you drive me absolutely insane. Your son has just met a nice girl with a solid work ethic and a goal in life. She's smart and driven, and if you must know, she wasn't at all sure about dating David because she didn't want to lose her focus. I'm just curious. Has there been a woman born who would get your approval?"

Hannah looked as though she wanted to cry. "Oh, no, am I really that bad?"

I patted her hand. "You love your son, and you want the best for him. I understand that. But you've got to let him go."

She stared at her coffee, and I thought I might have gone too far. But it needed to be said, and Hannah needed to hear it. "Is she really nice?"

"From what I've seen, I'd have been delighted if one of my sons had brought her home."

"Then I'll give her a chance."

I grinned at her. "I'm not sure you'll have much choice. David's pretty smitten."

She smiled. "He was so happy this evening, he was walking on air. I miss having that feeling myself."

"It's not too late for you, too, you know," I said. "You should try dating again."

"I'm a magnet for disastrous choices, and you know it."

"I admit you've met a few duds since I've known you."

She laughed, which was a good sign. "A few? That's being generous, and you know it."

"So the odds are with you to meet someone great," I said. "You'll never know if you don't try."

"Now who's speaking in platitudes?" she asked.

"Guilty as charged," I said.

A voice behind me said, "You're out late, aren't you?"

I didn't even have to turn around to see that it was Sheriff Hodges. "I didn't know you were keeping track of my movements."

"Well, now you know."

"You can't be serious," I said as I stood to face him.

My voice was hard and loud, but I didn't care who heard me. "I'm innocent."

"So you say."

"Is that why you're here, to harass me?"

He laughed without humor. "I'm here to tell you to leave my wife alone."

"You can't make me," I said, reverting to a childhood retort.

"Don't bet on it." He paid for his coffee and left.

Hannah said softly, "That man's not particularly fond of you, is he?"

"I don't know. I think he is deep down inside, but he's just hiding it."

"If he's that good, then he should hide the eggs at Easter for the kids."

I saw Hannah's concerned expression. "Don't worry about the sheriff. He's more bark than bite."

"I wouldn't be too sure of that."

Our coffees were gone, and I asked Hannah, "Would you like another one? It's my treat this time."

"Thanks, but I'd better run. I'm still wading through those essays."

"Okay, then we'll meet again tomorrow morning. I just have to grab a bowl of soup and then I'll be ready to go."

"I thought you already ate," she said.

"This is for Kendra. Herman told me she was under the weather."

"Well, aren't you a sweetheart?"

"I like to think so," I said. I could have told her my real motivation, but why not let her think I had the heart of a saint?

Hannah nodded. "I'll see you tomorrow then. And

Carolyn, thanks for the talk. I know it's not easy telling someone the truth."

"If I can't be brutally honest with you, who can?"

Outside, we split up, and I carried the soup back to Kendra's place.

I knocked on the front door, but Kendra didn't answer. "Kendra? Can I come in?" Was she asleep? I had this soup, and even if I couldn't talk to her, the least I could do was leave it for her to eat when she woke up. I tried the door, and it opened at my touch. A light was on in the hallway, so there was enough illumination for me to see my way into the kitchen. As I put the soup on the counter, I saw something that made my heart freeze.

It was an awl from my pottery shop—its handle stained with clay slip—nearly identical to the one that had killed Betty Wickline. It was hard to believe, but it looked like Kendra Williams *had* killed Betty. Why else would she have a duplicate of the murder weapon in her kitchen? The shaft had been wiped clean, but a trace of dark red still stained it, and the dish towel nearby was tainted as well. It looked like blood to me. So who had Kendra used this one on?

I started for the front door, but then I heard something from the bedroom. For a second I considered going back there, but then common sense slapped me in the face. Let the sheriff deal with Kendra. I was getting out of there.

That's when a hand clamped down on my shoulder. "Where are you going, Carolyn?"

"Herman? Keep your voice down. I don't want Kendra to hear us. What are you still doing here?"

"I haven't been here the whole time," he admitted as he peered out the window. "Where is he?"

"Who are you talking about?"

"The sheriff," he said as he continued to look outside.

There was something different about him, and I couldn't put my finger on it, but I didn't like the tone of his voice.

"We've got to get out of here," I said. "It's dangerous."

"What are you talking about?"

"Kendra. I think she killed Betty."

A look of relief spread over his face, followed by a burst of amusement. "Is that what you think?"

"I know it," I lied. Herman's expression had given him away. I'd narrowed the killer down to one of two people—which wasn't bad considering how many suspects I'd started out with—and now I realized how close I'd come to the truth.

Herman realized it, too. In a blur of motion he made a lightning grab for the awl, and before I could get out the door, he had the sharp, skewered tip at my throat.

"I gave you way too much credit," he said. "I thought you had it figured out when I saw you talking to the sheriff at the coffee shop."

"You followed me there?"

"I've been tailing you for days. When Bill was watching you from the shadows, I was watching both of you. You made it too easy."

"But why focus on me?" My mind was racing, searching for something I could use as a weapon. I had the diamond-shaped clay in my pocket, but could I use the sharp edge in my defense? Not while I had an awl at my throat. But if he let up for even a second, I might have a chance. It was my only hope.

"I had a suspicion you knew I was using your shop for my trysts with Betty. I couldn't take any chances. We only used it twice, but I know how nosy you are, and I was afraid you'd figure it out." He frowned. "It killed me to throw a brick through my own window, but I had to throw you off my trail."

"Why didn't you use your own place?"

"You saw where I've been living. Not even Betty was willing to meet me there, and she rarely let me come to her place. You had a couch, and I had a key. It was that simple."

"Why did you have to hide your relationship in the first place?"

Herman's ears grew red. "She wasn't all that keen on being seen with me. Can you believe that?"

"Is that why you killed her?" I had to stall, but I was running out of questions. Where was that blasted sheriff when I needed him?

He shrugged. "It was sort of an accident. Things got a little out of hand when she dumped me. I tried to talk her out of kicking me to the curb, but she'd already made up her mind."

I couldn't believe he was actually justifying the murder. It was time to change the subject. I didn't want him thinking about homicide at the moment. "So *you* left the note for her. I found it at her place."

Herman nodded. "I was counting on it turning up, but I didn't expect you'd be the one to find it. I threw the note on the floor after I came across it. It's not like it had my name on it, and I was hoping it might keep the sheriff's suspicion off me. I tore up the whole house searching for something I knew Betty had, but it wasn't the note I was after. Some idiot started rattling the front doorknob, and I had to get out of there before I was able to find what I was really looking for."

"So, did she get her extra money from you?" I had to keep drawing him out.

"Are you out of your mind? It was going to be the

other way around. I wanted to cut myself in on some of her action."

"I don't get it."

Herman shook his head. "The evidence she was using as leverage was what I was really searching for when I was there."

"Leverage? For what?"

He grinned. "Betty liked to spice up her life with a touch of blackmail. I found out when I was going through her closet one night while she was asleep. She caught me—that's why we didn't go to her place anymore. She said she didn't trust me. Can you believe that? There was enough for both of us, but she wouldn't share. As a matter of fact, that's probably the real reason she broke up with me."

"You never loved her at all, did you?"

"Does it matter? We were convenient for each other, that's about it. But that didn't mean she could just throw me away like that. She had to pay for what she did. You know what's funny? When I came back to look for her evidence, somebody else must have beaten me to it. It was already gone." He glanced out the window again, then said, "That's enough chatter. It's time to get this over with."

"Aren't you afraid Kendra is going to hear us?"

"I already took care of her. I had a devil of time getting the awl clean again."

"Why did you have to kill her?" I couldn't believe that she was dead.

"Apparently she's a lot smarter than you are. She figured it out on her own, and she threatened to go to the police. I didn't have any choice, so I had to get rid of her."

"Too bad you botched the job." Kendra stood in the

bedroom doorway. The front of her muumuu was heavily stained with blood. Yet somehow she found the strength to throw an ashtray toward us. Herman spun around, pointing the awl toward Kendra. It was the opening I'd been waiting for. I took the diamond-shaped piece of pottery out of my pocket and jabbed it as hard as I could into the back of his neck. It wasn't enough to do serious damage, but it must have hurt like the devil. Herman started clawing for it, but he couldn't reach it. While he was busy trying to extricate it, I picked up the nearest chair and brought it crashing down on his head.

As he slumped to the ground, Kendra said, "I wish you hadn't done that."

"I shouldn't have hit him?" Had she lost her mind?

"Not with that. It was the only genuine antique I had in here."

And then she fell face forward, landing squarely on top of the murderer.

I wasn't sure who was angrier with me, Bill or the sheriff. They were both yelling at me at the police station; finally, I'd had enough. "Stop it, you two. I keep telling you, I didn't do anything wrong."

Bill said, "You don't call going to Kendra's by yourself the wrong thing to do?"

"I was taking her soup," I said. There was no way I was going to admit to either one of them that I'd suspected her of murder. "How is she, by the way?"

Hodges said, "Her size worked in her favor. Herman didn't hit anything vital, but she probably would have bled to death if you hadn't come along when you did." He turned to Bill and asked, "Can I have a second alone with your wife?"

Bill looked at me, and I nodded. After Bill was gone, the sheriff said, "I just wanted to say that I'm sorry."

"About anything in particular, or just in general?"

"You're not going to make this easy on me, are you?"

"Not if I can help it. You haven't exactly been making my life rosy lately." I was a little jittery from the confrontation with Herman, but I was finally starting to wrap my head around the concept that my landlord was a murderer. How could I stay where I was? Fire at Will was home, and I hated to move. One thing I knew for sure. No matter what happened, I was getting a new couch.

"Yeah, well, that's why I'm sorry."

Bill knocked on the door before I could answer. "Are you two about finished up in there?"

"Just a second," I said, then turned to the sheriff. "And I'm sorry for not trusting you more than I did."

"Can't say I blame you," he said. "Let's just call it a truce, okay?"

"I can live with that."

There was a pounding on the door, then my husband called out, "Carolyn, are you all right?"

"I'm fine, Bill. For goodness sake, if I knew you were going to be such a baby about it, I would have let you stay."

"I was just worried about you," he said as I let him back in.

I kissed him soundly, then said, "That's why I keep you around. Let's go home." I turned to the sheriff and asked, "Is that okay with you?"

"Sure," he said. "And Carolyn, try to stay out of trouble, will you?"

"I'll do my best, but I can't make any promises. Trouble seems to find me wherever I go."

"Then it'll have to look at home," Bill said, "because that's where we're going right now."

The only thing worse than having Kendra suspect me of being a murderer was Kendra thinking I'd saved her life. No matter how many times I tried to tell her that we'd saved each other, she steadfastly refused to believe it.

It was almost enough to make me think about committing a little murder myself.

I couldn't have been more surprised when the Firing Squad threw me a party the next night at Fire at Will. There was food everywhere, and the best part was, the place was starting to feel like home again now that the murder tainting the place had been solved.

"Tell us how you figured it out again," Sandy asked.

"It all happened so quickly," I said. I wasn't about to tell them how long it had taken me to make the connection between my former landlord and the murder.

Martha asked, "What was the blackmailing all about? Did you ever find out what Betty knew?"

I looked at Butch and waited for him to answer, but he met my gaze with a shrug. When I realized he wasn't going to say anything, I said, "I guess we'll never know." Once again, I wondered just how reformed Butch really was. On the other hand, did I really want to know?

"All that really matters is that you're safe," Jenna said.

"And that we've put this all behind us," I replied. "I appreciate the sentiment, but I'm fine, honestly I am."

David said, "If that's the case, why don't we do something new, since we're all here? Does anyone have any ideas?"

"I'd like to learn how to make that face jug you did," Butch said, ready to pounce on anything that dropped the current line of conversation.

David looked at me and grinned. "What do you say? It's your shop."

I glanced at the Firing Squad—my circle of true friends—and realized that there was nothing in the world that I'd like more.

❧Clay-crafting Tips❧

Making Carolyn's Wind Ornaments

Carolyn's wind ornaments are easy to create yourself and add a nice touch of whimsy to any tree branch. They also make great additions for the wrapping of any gift, giving a real splash of class to packages wherever you use them. I like to make my own personalized wind ornaments every year to use at home and to give as simple, inexpensive gifts.

You don't need a potter's kiln, or any other special equipment, to make these ornaments. Polymer clay—the Sculpey brand for example—will do wonderfully. This clay is readily available at craft stores everywhere and comes in a variety of colors so you don't have to paint the finished product. When the clay is baked in your oven, it becomes rock hard. You can use your own cookie cutters on the material, and they yield beautiful results.

Knead the polymer clay and roll it out to a quarter of an inch thick. Then take your favorite cookie cutters and simply cut out the shapes you like. I prefer using heavy plas-

tic cutters when I do this, since they hold their shape and
don't deflect under the pressure. Cutters come in many different sizes and shapes, and they're inexpensive, too.

I also like to add textures to some of my shapes and
leave others unadorned. Round ornaments are especially
nice to embellish. Adding layers of wavy lines and color-
ful stars helps create variety. Using different colors of clay
will give your ornaments even more life and dimension.

After you're happy with your designs, simply punch a
hole in one corner of the ornament and bake them in your
main oven, or a toaster oven if you'd prefer. Once the ornaments bake and cool, they're hard and ready to use.

If you're making the ornaments with regular potter's
clay and a kiln, follow the steps above with regular clay,
then bisque-fire the ornaments after you've rolled them out
and cut the shapes. After that, paint or glaze your pieces
however you'd like. When you're finished with the second
firing, you have something special—handcrafted, inexpensive, and easy to create ornaments. Most importantly,
they're ready to share!